The Cabin

in the

Deep Dark

Woods

II Corinthians 3:3

Tim Barber

The Cabin
in the
Deep Dark
Woods

A Discerner of the Heart

Tim Barker

The Cabin in the Deep Dark Woods
Published by Tim Barker
Published in New Port Richey, FL 34654, U.S.A.

ISBN 978-1-951615-00-0
Library of Congress Control Number: 2020911666
Copyright © 2020 By Timothy L. Barker
Cover Design at date of publication: Tim Barker
Cover Photo at date of publication: David Gylland
Editor: Bonnie Olsen

Dedication

This book is dedicated to my wife Jilean, our four grown children, and our two grandchildren. Secondly, it is dedicated to the ministry of David Ursin of Making Jesus Known.

Making Jesus Known—Mission Statement: David has a heart to hold large scale evangelistic crusades throughout the earth where the truth of the Gospel will be clearly presented, and people will have the opportunity to fully surrender their lives to Jesus Christ.

I will be donating 25% of the profits from the sale of this book to Making Jesus Known. You can support David's ministry by purchasing additional copies and giving them to your family, friends, and co-workers.

To donate to **"Making Jesus Known,"** visit their website: https://makingjesusknown.org

George Whitefield

...I take it for granted you believe religion to be an inward thing; you believe it to be a work in the heart, a work wrought in the soul by the power of the Spirit of God.
~ George Whitfield

Table of Contents

Preface

I was inspired to write this story while listening to Jonathan Edwards's 1741 sermon *Sinners in the Hands of an Angry God.* Afterward, I thought, "Someone needs to write a story where God shows a group of people who they really are from His perspective." Jonathan Edwards's sermon and George Whitfield's 1741 sermon *The Method of Grace*—preached that people must be born again. Whether or not you have been born again, this book will challenge your theology by opening the Bible, presenting God's truth to your heart.

*Matthew 7:21 "Not everyone who says to Me, 'Lord, Lord,' shall enter the kingdom of heaven, **but he who does the will of My Father in heaven.** (22) "Many will say to Me in that day, 'Lord, Lord, have we not prophesied in Your name, cast out demons in Your name, and done many wonders in Your name?' (23) "And then I will declare to them, 'I never knew you; depart from Me, you who practice lawlessness!'*

Have you ever wondered where you will spend eternity? According to the Bible, it will either be heaven or hell. It's actually a bit more technical, but that's the central idea. A major theme of this book is avoiding the words—DEPART FROM ME. Once Jesus says those words to you, it's all over, and you are hell-bound forever. In other words, it's a one-way ticket to eternal torment in the flame of fire. Call it hell or the lake of fire—any way you spell it, it's going to hurt forever. This book was written so that you will have the opportunity to avoid hearing those horrible words— depart from Me. Instead, the words you should desire to hear Jesus say when you stand before Him in the next life are—"well done good and faithful servant" (Matthew 25:23).

Ezekiel 36:25 "Then I will sprinkle clean water on you, and you shall be clean; I will cleanse you from all your filthiness and from all your idols.

Ezekiel 36:25 is a good indicator of your eternal placement. Have you been cleansed from all your filthiness? Lastly: *Revelation 21:27 But there shall by no means enter it anything that defiles, or causes an abomination or a lie, but only those who are written in the Lamb's Book of Life.*

If you haven't been cleansed from all your filthiness, how will you enter a place (heaven/the New Jerusalem) that forbids anything that defiles? I hope you enjoy your stay at the Cabin in the Deep Dark Woods. Please be sure to visit again when the next book is published—*The Spirit and the Bride.*

Sincerely,

Tim Barker

December 2020

Acknowledgments

I want to thank my wife, Jilean Barker, for reviewing this book and being my greatest supporter. I want to thank my mother and father for raising me in a Christian home. God was freely and openly discussed, leading me to have a firm foundation to fall on when I was ready to turn my life over to Jesus Christ. I want to thank John and Annette Murray, who helped with the editing process. They provided their input early, even before all the chapters were finalized. I want to thank Pastors Susan and Ken Pippin for their assistance and review. And finally, Bonnie Olsen, for her patience during her review, she put in a lot of work. Thank you all.

About this Book

The Cabin in the Deep Dark Woods may be read several ways. First, like any book, front to back. Secondly, read each chapter and answer the discussion questions. Thirdly, read each chapter, answer the discussion questions, and review all scriptures listed at the end of the chapter, or any way that you choose. Some of the Discussion Questions have answers provided and are denoted with the word (Answer). On occasion, a chapter will have a (Scripture Section:). Those scriptures are not found in that chapter.

You will want to pay particular attention to the following: *Without spoiling the story, italics are used to indicate a transition is occurring during the story that the character or characters are aware of. Italics are also utilized in the front matter and the appendix sections to indicate scripture.* **Bold type is utilized when something important is said or happens, and if it is missed, the reader may not catch what follows. It is used in some chapters as a subject header or a time transition header. You will also see bold type in the front matter and the appendix section to highlight a point.** Some chapters use offset indentation to tell a story or bring out a thought. Next to most chapter headings there is a day of the week, e.g. (Chapter 1 ~ Friday). That chapter occurred on that day of the week. Whenever a day of the week is not shown in the chapter heading, that chapter occurred at another time, before or after the trip to the cabin. At the end of some sentences and paragraphs, there are scripture references in parentheses, e.g. (John 3:16). This will allow you to verify the content of that sentence or paragraph. Some places have multiple references as the sentence or paragraph was detailed. When looking up these scripture references, if a connection CANNOT be made, check to ensure you are reading the correct passage. Throughout this book, quotations indicate that a character is speaking—colons (:) are utilized to indicate a long character quotation. On a few occasions, I have used curly brackets {…}. The scriptures contained within are closely associated with each other. Example: {Joel 1:1 & 2:28-32, Acts 2:17-21}. Finally, all names utilized in this book are fictitious and are in no way implied to represent a real person.

There are four appendixes (A through D) at the back of this book. For example, you will find in chapter 1: (See appendix A for the remainder of the message from Matthew 7:21-23). The information contained in the appendix would not keep with the flow of the story.

This is a fictitious work, and in no way is it intended to override anything contained in scripture. All things contained in this book are superseded by the Bible. After you finish this book, I strongly encourage you to read your Bible, beginning in the book of John. And please don't forget to use this book as a study guide. It could also be used as a family devotional or a group study. Finally, enjoy your new book and look for others written by Tim Barker in which the story revolves around the same places in Edwardsville: the cabin, the mine, and the ranger station.

Thank you for purchasing *The Cabin in the Deep Dark Woods*. As a special gift I would like to send you a free PDF of *The Minister of the Holy Spirit*, a 90-day study of the scriptures. I like to call it the Holy Spirit on training wheels. Just send an email to:
TheCabin@turnifyouwill.org
TheCabinInTheDeepDarkWoods.com
Thank you
Tim Barker

Chapter 1 ~ Friday

The Journey Begins

I want to tell you a story about a group of kids whose lives were changed many years ago while visiting a cabin one weekend in late autumn. This trip started out on a typical Friday morning and promised to give everyone some hiking, some exploring, and some well-needed relaxation. However, what occurred on that trip was nothing short of an adventure. This is the account of how it all transpired.

As the group was hiking along the first marked trail making their way to the cabin, two of the boys fell behind the others. As Peter Myers and Mark Phillips talked to each other, they became captivated by the scenery and the beauty of nature all around them. They saw the hills and the valleys with the mountain peaks in the background. Suddenly, there was a man wearing a hooded cloak with his face concealed that looked very similar to a hooded man from a gas station earlier that same day. He began following them, having his face veiled. Realizing that they had fallen behind the others, the two boys decided to take a short cut along an unmarked trail. There they were met by another man, wearing a hooded cloak with his face also veiled. The first hooded man called them by name, saying, "Eyes sees you, eyes sees you, Peter Myers. Eyes sees you, eyes sees you, Mark Phillips. Come to me, and I will give you a treasure that will enlighten you and your friends." Peter and Mark started to walk back the way they had come, but the second hooded man blocked their way. Mark yelled to Peter, "RUN!" As both boys begin to run further and further into the deep dark woods down the unmarked trail, fear began to grip their very being. There is a type of fear that prevents a person from screaming for help, and it is terrifying. This type of fear gripped both boys. Peter and Mark were caught in between those two hooded men and were trying to escape.

Clark Williams, one of the youth leaders, felt the need to do an on the march headcount as he sensed that something was wrong. He counted, again and again, not letting anyone else know that he had been short on the headcount twice or perhaps even five times. With a slight panic in his voice, Clark yelled, "WHO'S MISSING?! WHO IS MISSING?!" Brenda Summers looked around and said, "It's Peter and Mark!" And at once, everyone stopped and began to yell for them. Jill Williams, Clark's wife and co-leader, was thinking to herself, "This can't be happening, this just can't be happening!" "PETER, MARK, WHERE ARE YOU TWO?!" Everyone yelled in unison, without an answer as to their whereabouts.

Eight Hours Earlier at Peter Myers's Home

It was early Friday morning, and Senior Pastor James Myers began to prepare his Sunday morning message as he had done every week for the past seven years. He had been following an outline on the Holy Spirit and was nearly three-quarters of the way through it. He thought that he was ready for something else to preach on. He said to himself, "I'm not sure if I want to preach on the Holy Spirit anymore. I'm just not feeling it." Afterward, he caught himself looking around his study, peering down the hallway and thinking to himself, "I hope I didn't say that out loud! No one wants a pastor who is burnt out preaching on the Holy Spirit and a senior pastor at that." Then he said out loud, "Of course, no one wants to hear that." Peter thought he heard his dad and yelled from the other room, "Did you say something, Dad?" Pastor James answered, "No, I was just talking to myself, never mind me." Then Pastor James said to himself, "Okay, James, you have to keep all that burn out stuff to yourself, buddy, there are no other jobs out there for you. Nobody wants to hire an old charred pastor." "Hey, Dad, I'm going to load my gear into the truck. Can we leave soon? Oh, and remember you said that you would take me to get a sandwich on the way to the church," Peter said.

At that, Pastor James broke his pencil. He mumbled something under his breath as he yelled back across the house, "I'll be just a few more minutes to finish this thought," as several of his church problems were raging through his mind. "Okay, no problem, just remember the church van leaves at 10:00 a.m. sharp." Peter reminded his dad, not knowing that it was beginning to irritate him. "Got it," said Pastor James with a cynical undertone that only he caught. "Hey, Dad," Peter said, once again yelling across the house, "did I tell you that Mark was coming over, and we are giving him a ride to the church?" Once again, Pastor James held in his emotions with a slightly cynical undertone by saying to his son, "No problem, Peter." And while throwing his arms up in the air, he added under his breath, "I've got all day to get this sermon ready for the Sunday morning service. I can run kids all over town, no problem. I just hope my congregation appreciates all that I do for this church."

Mark Phillips and his grandmother arrived at the Myers's home. Peter ran outside and gave his best friend a high five and then helped him load his camping gear into the truck. Mark said to Peter, "This trip is going to be so good. I've been looking forward to it for a long time." They made their way into the house after the last of the camping gear was stowed away in the truck.

Pastor James was speaking with Mark's grandmother, Gertrude Phillips, in the kitchen. "Good morning Mrs. Phillips," he said, "here's my phone number if there is anything you need while Mark is away on his trip," handing her his business card. "Why thank you, Pastor, I really appreciate this," said Mrs. Phillips. She said that while holding his business card up to the light and staring at it. "Gertrude. Gertrude! Mrs. Phillips?!" Pastor James finally gained the attention of Mark's grandmother. He said, "Ma'am, I can assure you that it's my business card." Mrs. Phillips quickly took it down and put it in her coat pocket. "Oh dear, oh dear, I'm so sorry, I couldn't see it clearly," she said, acting a little confused.

It was during that time Peter and Mark entered the kitchen. Mark remembered that his grandmother had not been acting herself lately. Peter gave Mark a look as if to say, is everything alright with your grandmother? Just then, Stacy Myers entered the room, not knowing what had transpired a moment ago and said, "Hey dear, don't you think it's time you get these two young lads on the road, so they can get to the church?" Pastor James answered, "I'm sorry, Mrs. Phillips, I will need to be going." As he walked away, he rolled his eyes at his wife. Not looking at the two boys, Pastor James headed to the truck saying in a slight huff, "Let's get this show on the road." He was still questioning his wife's logic that he had time to take the boys to the church.

Jill Williams had gotten up bright and early to get the final odds and ends packed for the retreat that weekend. She made sure that she and her husband Clark had the reservation paperwork for the cabin packed in one of their bags, which was the responsibility of the youth group leaders. "Clark, you need to get up. We should be leaving in the next few minutes. Clark! CLARK! Did you hear me? Clark, would you please get up now?!" Jill said sternly as her frustration and anxiety were making their way to the surface. Clark rolled out of bed and headed to the kitchen. He asked her, "Jill, did you make coffee this morning?" "NO, and you don't have time to either," she answered. Then she asked, "Did you pack your backpack yet?" Clark responded to his wife's question by gesturing with his backpack holding it up, indicating that it was packed and ready to go. Clark said, "By the way, I filled the gas tank, got the oil changed, and had the tires rotated on the church van so we can leave the church as soon as all the kids are loaded up." Jill gave him a look that said, I can't believe you made coffee. Then she said, "There wasn't enough time, you should have gotten up an hour ago." Clark grabbed his backpack and coffee mug, thinking that she's the one that should have made it in the first place. He walked past his wife, picked up her bag, and asked her, "Is your bag ready?" He headed to the car with Jill following, and she locked the door behind them.

On the way to the church, Pastor James stopped at the Old Horse Thief Hamburger Stand to get a burger for himself and the boys. While standing in line, Mark asked Peter in a whisper, "Is your dad alright? He doesn't seem to be himself lately. I mean, he's different at church. Is everything okay at home?" "What will you boys be ordering today?" asked the cashier. Peter used that moment to evade the question from Mark, ignoring his best friend. Pastor James said to her, "Three hamburgers, three orders of french fries, and three sodas—oh and to go." He didn't even stop to consider that the boys may want to order something different. After all, they were high school students, not little children anymore. Pastor James was quiet while the order was prepared. Mark took advantage of that time to reiterate the question. He looked into his best friend's eyes, asking the question once more, sensing that something was just not right about Peter's dad. "Yeah, he's been a little bit cranky and irritable lately, that's for sure. I'm definitely ready for this trip," said Peter, seeming a little embarrassed having said that about his dad. "Order number 430. Sir, is your ticket 430?" asked the cashier. "Oh yes," said Pastor James. He paid for the order and headed to the door, not looking back to see if the two boys were coming with him. "Hey, we better go, your dads leaving without us," Mark said, grabbing Peter's arm and heading for the door.

Pastor James was driving to the Truth Valley Church while the radio played on 91.5 the ROCK FM. "Hey, everyone out there in radio land," said the D.J., Rex Redman, loudly. Pastor James turned the volume down a bit. "I'm glad you're all here listening to the ROCK FM. I've got a special guest speaker today, Pastor Melvin Baldwin, from Southland Bible College," said Rex, introducing him. Pastor Baldwin began his message by saying: "Thank you, Rex, I always love being a part of the ROCK FM. Today I'm going to speak to you from Matthew 7:21-23. In this passage, we find there will be some people, even members of local churches, that will one day stand before Jesus Christ and have those horrible words spoken to them, 'depart from Me.' It was clear that Jesus was speaking to people who thought they were saved but were never truly converted. Who may these people be..." "CLICK" went the radio dial as Pastor James turned it off. Just then, Mark looked over at Peter, both boys wondered why Peter's dad turned the radio off since the guest speaker was just getting started with his message. Mark thought to himself, "Could I be one of those people?"

It was pretty quiet the rest of the way, and all three were consumed with eating their meal as Pastor James made his way to the church. However, Mark couldn't shake that question as it continued to play in his mind, "Who may these people be...?"

See appendix A for the remainder of the message from Matthew 7:21-23.

Discussion Questions:

1) Have you ever felt burnt out serving God like Senior Pastor James Myers displayed in this chapter?

2) Can you find any examples in the Bible where a situation like this was handled? What was the outcome?
   Answer: Peter's denial of Jesus and his subsequent restoration to apostleship: John 13:36-38, John 18:15-18, John 18:25-27, John 21:15-19.

3) Have you ever had a situation in your life where you were gripped with fear that had the power to isolate you from others who were able to keep you on the right path, like Peter and Mark in this chapter?

Scripture: Matthew 7:21-23.

Discussion Question Scriptures: John 13:36-38, John 18:15-18, John 18:25-27, John 21:15-19.

Chapter 2 ~ Friday

That Treasure Chest

S oon Pastor James arrived at the Truth Valley Church with Peter and Mark, and the others were arriving. The three Summers sisters, Brenda, Daisy, and Lisa, the youngest and their brother Brad were dropped off by their mother, Sara. She also gave Brenda's best friend, Becky Owens a ride. Andrew Jeremiah was the last of the kids to arrive at the church. Soon after, Mr. and Mrs. Williams, the youth leaders for that year's trip to the Cabin in the Deep Dark Woods, also arrived at the church. All the campers had loaded their camping gear into the van and were ready to go. Before they left, Peter said to Mark, "Hey, I'm sorry about how my dad's been acting; he's just not been himself lately."

"You all have fun on your trip and drive safely," Pastor James yelled as Clark was pulling the van out of the church parking lot. The sign on the back of the van said, "OFF TO THE CABIN WE GGGOOOOOOOOO!!" Clark looked over at his wife and said, "This is going to be an eye-opening trip for everyone." "You had better believe it," she replied. They could hear the kids in the back of the van singing out the church's motto, "Where the truth of the Spirit flows into the valley."

Soon the group made their first stop for gas on their six-hour drive to the cabin. Before anyone exited the van, Clark said to the group, "Be sure to use the buddy system." Peter and Mark teamed up and went around to the back of the gas station, where there was a scenic view from the mountain they were on. As the two boys went around the corner, they bumped into a man wearing a hooded cloak with his face concealed by a veil. He was walking in the other direction, toward the front of the gas station. Thinking no more about him, they viewed the other mountains that were all around them. The sun was illuminating all the beauty before their eyes. Soon they decided they should be heading back to the van. "All in, we're ready to rock and roll," Jill said, as the headcount was right on the money. She added with emphases, "We don't want to lose any of these children the Lord has given us" (Hebrews 2:10-18).

It was a few hours later when the church van pulled into the parking lot of the Cabin in the Way. Before anyone got out, Clark said to the kids, "Don't forget your gear, and above all else, remember, stay together." The long trek to the cabin was about to begin along the first marked trail. That cabin had been used by the Truth Valley Church for many years; it had even become a generational event. There were some kids on that trip whose parents had been to the cabin when they were young. **It's known as the Cabin in the Deep Dark Woods; that's what they called it at Truth Valley. It's really called the Cabin in the Way, a part of a larger property that belongs to the state parks department.** It was at this cabin that our story took place. I am about to tell you how a group of kids and their youth leader's lives were changed while visiting the Cabin in the Way on a much-needed retreat from everyday life. This trip started out on a typical Friday morning that promised to give everyone a bit of hiking, some exploring, and some well-needed rest. However, what occurred there was nothing short of an adventure. **This is how it all began as we rejoin our campers on their hike to the Cabin in the Deep Dark Woods.**

The main group of hikers was now in full panic mode and desperately searching for Peter and Mark. Clark was walking around in circles with his hands on his head, wondering how this situation could have happened. He heard his wife's voice piercing into that part of his brain that was controlling his panic. "Clark, you can't just stand there and think that you are going to find Peter and Mark like that, you have to do something, anything!" Jill said. Brad jumped into the conversation and said, "Mr. Williams, we could walk back the way we came and…" "That's perfect," Jill interrupted him, as she began leading the group back the way that they had come while pulling Clark along by his arm.

Once again, Peter and Mark found themselves running the other way to escape the two hooded men. Panic was flowing through their veins like ice water down a mountain stream in the springtime. Peter tripped over an old cypress stump, and Mark started to run back the way they came. Mark looked back, seeing Peter lying on the ground and knowing in his heart that he couldn't leave his best friend to face them alone. Mark turned around and ran back. After he grabbed Peter by the arm and helped him up, one of those hooded men stood in front of them, and the other was standing behind them.

The first hooded man once again said to the boys, "Eyes sees you, eyes sees you, Peter Myers. Eyes sees you, eyes sees you, Mark Philips. Come to me, and I will give you a treasure that will enlighten you and your friends." Peter and Mark looked at one another, not knowing how they could escape at that point. The first hooded man said, "Behold, I stand at the door and knock" (Revelation 3:20). Then he handed a treasure chest to Peter and said, "Remember to use the filter, it will be most helpful to you and your friends." Then the hooded men disappeared into the deep dark woods. Peter and Mark quickly made their way out of the short cut and caught up to the main group. Peter had buried the treasure chest deep within his backpack to hide it from the others.

"Hey, where were you two? We were just searching for you," Andrew said. "Welcome back, boys," Clark said, as he felt relieved by their safe return, and at the same time, his despair was vanishing away. "Now, let's get on with our hike before it gets dark." Clark made an emphasis on the fact that they had to make it to the cabin before sunset. As they walked along the first marked trail, a set of glowing eyes followed them, but no one noticed.

The group finally made their way to the cabin just as the sun was going down. The last light of day was vanishing, and a beautiful sunset was leaving its mark in the sky. "Well, that was close," Brad said as they all got into the cabin just before dark. Peter and Mark went back outside and were sitting on the stone wall in front of the cabin. Peter was still a little shaken-up by the encounter with the man wearing the hooded cloak. He said to Mark while he pulled the treasure chest out of his backpack, "What do you think about this treasure chest that dude gave me?" "I don't know, man," Mark replied, I would be afraid to open it tonight; let's just put it under your bed and forget about it. Maybe we can just leave it here in the cabin. Just don't tell anybody about what happened back there in the woods, nobody will believe us anyway." Peter replied, "That's for sure."

Once back inside the cabin, Peter and Mark saw Andrew, and he asked them, "Hey, where did you two guys get that treasure chest?" They tried to hide it, but Jill also saw it and said, "Wow, Peter, that's a beautiful treasure chest you have there." Turning around to look, Brad bumped into Peter's arm, causing him to drop the treasure chest on the hardwood floor. Then a brand-new state of the art video camera fell out. "Wow," said Brad, "where did you guys get that video camera? It must have cost a bazillion dollars; that thing is way cool!" Clark saw all the commotion and also the new video camera lying on the floor. "Peter," he asked, "where did you get that video camera? I don't remember you having it earlier today." Peter said, "It's a long story." "Yeah," said Mark interrupting, "it's a long story, and we're getting pretty tired, so maybe we can tell you all about it tomorrow." At that, the group began the process of retiring for the night.

Jill said, "It's going to be a big day tomorrow," referring to the annual hike to the Edwardsville Ranger Station. Jill was leading all the girls to their side of the cabin. She said, "We'll see you fellas in the morning, and don't forget to make breakfast." She was rubbing in the fact that the girls raised more money for that trip than the boys did—hence the loser of the wager had to cook breakfast for the entire retreat. Jill said, "Goodnight, all you egg heads. Don't forget to get cracking bright and early for our breakfast. I like mine over easy." The rest of the night was uneventful as everyone was tired. It had been a long day getting everything ready for the trip and then that twenty-minute hike to the cabin. All was quiet outside as the crickets played a tune that matched the tranquility of the wilderness view of the mountain range. There were, however, some men wearing hooded cloaks with eyes aglow watching over the cabin and those within.

Discussion Questions:

1) Do you have issues that are similar to what Peter and Mark were facing in this chapter? Mark said to Peter, "Just don't tell anybody about what happened back there in the woods; nobody will believe us anyway."

2) Is there a fear that a lie is better than the truth? If so, is there anyone that you could talk to about this behavior?

3) "Yeah," said Mark interrupting, "it's a long story, and we're getting pretty tired, so maybe we can tell you all about it tomorrow." Have you ever had a situation where you didn't want to be honest and then tried to manipulate those around you like Mark did in this chapter?

Scriptures: Hebrews 2:10-18, Revelation 3:20.

Discussion Question Scriptures: none.

Chapter 3 ~ Saturday

An Ancient Scroll

Beep—Beep—Beep. "WOULD YOU TURN THAT THING OFF AND MAKE MY BREAKFAST!" Jill said to Clark. She wasn't a big fan of her husband's alarm clock, especially when he slept through it. Jill could hear her husband murmuring under his breath about her comment. She was thinking about how things in their marriage weren't as good as most people thought. She put on her happy face and roused all the girls suggesting they get to the bathroom before the boys got up.

Breakfast went as planned, and clean up went fast as the girls pitched in so the day's activities could begin. "I'm so excited," Becky said, as she tucked her Bible under her arm. She sat at the kitchen table for that morning's devotional session, which Andrew led. Andrew held regular Bible studies at his public high school and had prepared a few lessons for that trip. Andrew started the lesson by saying, "Today's Bible lesson is from Hebrews 11:6, which says that without faith, it is impossible to please God." Andrew continued with his lesson, and all the kids felt they got something out of it. Though some thought he took the Bible too seriously for a high school kid. Some also wondered if he had intentions of being a pastor. His teachings seemed to have more substance than their own Senior Pastor's did at times. Becky and

Lisa were the first ones to leave the table, even before Andrew had a chance to end his lesson. Becky said to Lisa, "I just hate it when he talks about all that faith crap, I got enough faith anyway!"
See appendix B for the remainder of the lesson from Hebrews 11:6.

After that lesson by Andrew, the youth group had planned to take a hike along the second marked trail, over the red covered bridge, down to the ranger station. Every year the Truth Valley Church youth group would take a tour of the ranger station and the abandoned Edwardsville Mine and Millworks Company. It was this field trip that everyone had been looking forward to. Then Clark got everyone's attention and said, "We're going to start the day with our hike to the ranger station. Get your partners and team up, and remember, stay together!" He said that looking directly at Peter and Mark.

Peter and Mark had been best friends since grade school and were on the same little league baseball team for five years straight. Brenda always said about Peter and Mark, "You would think those two were brothers; you just can't separate them," she was the oldest of the Summers children. The Summers family lost their father Ricky from an illness and have struggled since. Soon after, they lost their house and were forced to get a government-subsidized apartment. Their mother Sara worked a lot of nights and missed church more often than not. Some even said she was a backslider, now that her husband was gone. But they always ended with, "bless her little heart for trying so hard." Well, that's the talk of the church at the Coffee Barn, where the gossip goes down, and the truth is never found.

The three older Summers children became aware of God when things were good at home, before their father got sick. On the other hand, Lisa became aware of God when her father, Ricky first became ill. The three older children had been grounded in God. They had a foundation, where Lisa, the youngest, never received that needed parental attention, and she fell by the wayside. She never received the foundation to develop a belief in God. As the months and years flew by, during Ricky's illness, Lisa became hardened by all the stress and the general lifestyle of the

Summers's household. Sara prayed daily for God to heal her husband. It was just over two years since Ricky started feeling bad until he passed away, and Lisa got lost in all that mess.

Once all the students had their hiking partners, they were off to the ranger station. As the group was hiking along the second marked trail, Clark pointed out some trees and some different kinds of foliage. There were some markers with a short description of the native species. "Look over there," Brad said, as he pointed out some wildlife down by the creek. The hike was uneventful as the group made their way to the ranger station, where they could officially check-in and turn in the reservation paperwork.

Halfway through the hike, Peter and Mark once again fell behind the others before anyone had a chance to make it to the red covered bridge. Suddenly, another hooded man appeared out of nowhere and said to them, "Eyes sees you, Peter Myers, and eyes sees you, Mark Phillips." They tried to run away from the hooded man, but another one came from behind and put a clay jar in Peter's hands. The first one said to Peter and Mark, "If anyone hears My voice and opens the door." Then the hooded man disappeared into the deep dark woods just as the second one walked back the way he came. Peter and Mark decided they needed to stay with the group because these hooded men were beginning to freak them out.

After a few minutes, they caught up to the group. Daisy asked, "Hey guys, what's in the clay jar?" She grabbed for it, causing it to open, dropping its contents on the ground in front of everyone. Andrew said, "Hey, that looks like an ancient scroll." Clark asked, "Where did you two boys get that?" Mark told him that they found it. He said that because he thought the truth would be too hard to explain. "Is that true, Peter?" asked Jill. "Well, yeah, kind of," said Peter. "Kind of?" asked Clark. Then he said, "First, a video camera falls out of a treasure chest, and now an ancient scroll falls out of a clay jar. What's going on, you two?" Peter said, "I'm just not sure?" Jill interrupted them, saying, "We should be heading back to the cabin now. I've noticed the clouds are starting to build to the north. I think a storm is coming our way." At that, the group headed quietly back to the Cabin in the Way. They were not able to make it to the ranger station that day. Everyone made it safely inside the cabin just as the first raindrop fell, and a thunderclap shouted a warning that this storm was going to be a fierce one.

Once inside, Jill and Clark started to get lunch ready while the kids put away their backpacks from the morning hike. After a few minutes of preparation, lunch was served. Jill rang the cowbell telling everyone to come and get it. Peter and Mark were still sitting on their beds and looking at the scroll while the others started eating their lunch.

"Hey, Peter, what does it say on the scroll?" Mark asked. Peter looked hard at the scroll and read the markings out loud, "It says Revelation 3:20." Mark asked, "Was that there before?" Peter replied, "No, I'm sure it wasn't. Grab that Bible, and let's look it up." Mark grabbed a Bible that was lying on the table, in-between the rows of beds, and read aloud. "Behold, I stand at the door and knock. If anyone hears My voice and opens the door, I will come into him and dine with him, and he with Me." "Whoa, whoa, whoa, stop right there, that's the same thing the hooded man said to us in the woods," Peter shouted. With that, he got the attention of the others who were eating lunch at the table, and they looked over at Peter and Mark. "Hey, that's my mom's Bible," Lisa said. "What do you mean, that's Mom's Bible. Our father gave that to her; you just can't take it on a camping trip!" Daisy said. Just then, Brad jumped up and grabbed the ancient scroll out of Peter's hand and said to Peter and Mark, "That wasn't written there before." He picked up his mother's Bible and read the scripture aloud for everyone to hear. Then Brad asked, "Mr. Williams, what does this scripture mean?" Clark looked at the group of teenagers, and the only thing that he knew about this verse was superficial at best, so he gave it a shot. He said, "Well, guys, this scripture, this verse, this passage in the Bible was written by the Apostle John to get our attention so that we can serve Jesus better. Yep… that's right, it was written so we can serve Him better." Clark thought he nailed that one. Then his head popped when Andrew said, "Uh, Mr. Williams, with all due respect." He reached for the open Bible of Mrs. Summers that was now laying on Mark's bed.

Andrew continued by saying: "This scripture is all about our Lord and Savior Jesus Christ being outside His church because the people inside want to do church their way. When the will of the Father (John 6:39-40) is not followed, Jesus is the one outside. When the scriptures are not followed, Jesus is the one outside; when prayer is dead, Jesus is outside. The only way to get Jesus back in the church is through true repentance and brokenness of the heart and spirit."

Jill said, looking directly at her husband, "Well, I guess someone hasn't been reading his Bible. Thank you, Andrew Jeremiah, for that interpretation." No one except Peter, Mark, and Brad noticed the scroll had Revelation 3:20 written on it. Brad looked hard at the two boys and said, "You better come clean and tell me what's going on here. Where did this Ancient scroll come from?!" So, Peter let Brad in on everything that happened on the trail with the hooded men, the video camera, and the ancient scroll. Brad said, "You two are starting to freak me out. So, let me get this straight, you two were on the trail when you encountered a..."

Just then, Brenda yelled, "HEY, PETER! Get your video camera; the storm is really getting bad! I see a tornado!" As Peter grabbed the video camera, he fumbled around while trying to turn it on, but he couldn't find the power button. Then suddenly, it came on by itself and began to film Brenda. As Peter watched through the video screen, it was extremely blurry, with two shadows on either side of her. "I can't see anything," Peter said to Mark. **Just then, Mark remembered the words of the first hooded man from the woods, "Remember to use the filter; it will be most helpful to you and your friends."** Mark reminded Peter about the filter and the words of the hooded man. Then Peter found the filter dial and turned it all the way to the right. As Peter looked up from the camera video screen, he couldn't believe what he saw outside; the storm lifted away, the tornado vanished, and the sun came out just like a brand-new day. Peter was again fixed on the camera's screen. Then Brenda and her two sisters became visible after he adjusted the filter dial. Peter motioned for Brad to look at the camera screen with him. Jill came around to watch and said, "Turn up the volume," then the volume turned up on its own. Brenda, Daisy, and Lisa were all clearly visible on the camera view screen. A voice began to speak, saying, "The kingdom of heaven is like ten young virgins."

Discussion Questions:

1) Have you used gossip in the past to feed the grapevine of information enabling others to have a form of the truth?

2) Do you know anyone who uses lies like Mark did when he said they found the ancient scroll because he thought the truth would be too hard to explain?

3) Hebrews 11:6 says, But without faith, it is impossible to please God. Where is your faith? Have you prayed lately? Do you read your Bible daily?

4) Are there things in your life that are not as people around you think, like the Williams's marriage? The Holy Spirit is a discerner of the thoughts and intents of the heart, Hebrews 4:12. What is Jesus thinking about you right now? Are you comfortable with the judgment of Jesus Christ in your life?

Scriptures: Hebrews 11:6, Revelation 3:20, John 6:39-40.

Discussion Question Scriptures: Hebrews 11:6, Hebrews 4:12.

Chapter 4 ~ Saturday

The Wise Took Oil

The camera displayed all on its own all three of the Summers sisters on the video screen. Then the voice of an angel was heard narrating what the three girls were doing. The camera continued to play out the scene of the young virgins.

All three Summers sisters were seen on the viewscreen as if they were in a movie. The video camera viewed them from the perspective of God, how that they were actually known by Jesus, and the Holy Spirit revealed who they really were spiritually.

The kingdom of heaven is like ten young virgins, which took their lamps and went out to meet the Bridegroom. Five of them were wise, among them were Brenda and Daisy. And five were foolish, among them was Lisa. The foolish ones took their lamps and brought no oil with them, but the wise took oil in their containers with their lamps. While the Bridegroom was delayed, they all slept. At midnight there was a cry made, "Behold, the Bridegroom comes, go out to meet Him." Then all the virgins arose and made their lamps ready. The foolish virgins said to the wise, "Please give us some of your oil, for our lamps are gone out." But the wise answered, saying, "No, there won't be enough for us and you, go to them who sell, and buy for yourselves."

While they went to buy, the Bridegroom came. And those who were ready went in with Him to the wedding, and the door was shut. Afterward, the foolish virgins came, saying, "Lord, open to us." But he answered and said, "I can assure you, I don't know you." Watch and be alert, for you do not know the day nor the hour when the Son of Man is coming (Matthew 25:1-13).

The three Summers sisters were watching in shock and horror as Lisa was given the verdict that she was one of the foolish virgins, which the Bridegroom did not know.

And the smoke of her torment ascends forever and ever. She will have no rest day or night (Revelation 14:11). At this point, everyone in the group was watching, and they saw Lisa being cast into the Lake of Fire on the video screen. She was wholly engulfed in the flame of the fire that burns forever and ever. Lisa was heard belting out screams that did not sound human in origin. Just before the camera screen went blank, Lisa was heard utterly despising God with blasphemies that were directed towards Him and His nature. Shouting out words so hideous, no one could imagine that a human could be so depraved. Having no hope of escaping her torments, her entire being hated God. Knowing instantly, the lake of fire was her new home, her eternal residence, and that the fire would never cease to torment her day and night, year after year, century after century, endlessly. Then the video camera shut off, and the screams of Lisa seemed to linger in the cabin for a few moments longer.

The Summers children gathered around Lisa and consoled her as the video was very graphic. It depicted that she had not been born again when the Lord Jesus came calling. Brenda looked at her sister Daisy and asked, "Could it be possible that Lisa has never been born again?" Daisy looked at Lisa, who was now sitting on the cabin floor, and asked her, "Lisa, have you ever accepted Jesus Christ as your personal savior?" Lisa looked up and said in a humble mannerism, "I don't know, maybe not. I said a prayer once, or maybe even twice, I'm not sure anymore. I just don't understand how to be saved." Then with tears flowing, Lisa began to weep and cry out, displaying utter brokenness as she called upon the name of the Lord Jesus.

Lisa said, "Lord, I have never given You place in my life, and I want to change that right now. I want You to be my Savior and my Lord." Lisa began to confess her sins to Jesus Christ. Those in the cabin felt the brokenness of her spirit. This went on for quite some time with lots of tears. Then after that, Lisa fell into the arms of her siblings, saying there was a peace that had come over her that she could not describe in words. It was the very opposite of what had been expressed in the video. Then the camera turned back on by itself, and Brad was seen by all on the camera screen.

Discussion Questions:

1) Have you considered what it would be like to spend a week burning in hell or the lake of fire? How about a month or even a year? Do you feel that you could stand burning in the lake of fire for all eternity?

2) This concept of eternal torment is not appealing. Would you give your life over to Jesus, in this life, so that the promises of the Bible would be your sure reward rather than your eternal regrets? John 3:16 For God so loved the world that He gave His only begotten Son, that whoever believes in Him should not perish but have everlasting life.

3) Try reading from the Amplified version: John 3:16 For God so [greatly] loved and dearly prized the world, that He [even] gave His [One and] only begotten Son, so that whoever believes and trusts in Him [as Savior] shall not perish, but have eternal life. [AMP]

4) Where did Jesus declare hell to be a real place?
   Answer: Mark 9:42-48, Matthew 13:41-43, Luke 16:19-31.

5) Where does the Bible speak on rewards?
   Answer: Revelation 22:12 & II Corinthians 5:9-11. There are others if you care to search them out.

Scriptures: Matthew 25:1-13, Revelation 14:11.

Discussion Question Scriptures: John 3:16, Mark 9:42-48, Matthew 13:41-43, Luke 16:19-31, Revelation 22:12, II Corinthians 5:9-11.

Chapter 5 ~ Saturday

In the Spirit it's Supposed to Click

Becky said, "The focus is a little fuzzy." She was still astonished by Lisa's camera episode. Then Peter slowly turned the filter dial to the right, bringing the camera into focus, and then Brad was seen clearly by all on the view screen. This was not what he did with the Summers sisters; he had moved the filter dial fast with them. By moving the filter dial slowly, everyone could see a transition from the flesh nature of man to the spirit nature of God. Then Andrew had a thought, so he went to get Mrs. Summers's Bible. As he picked it up, a church bulletin fell out onto the floor and went under a bed, unknown to everyone in the room. Then Andrew read from II Kings 6:14-18, where the Syrian Army surrounded Israel with horses and chariots in great numbers. Elisha prayed to God that He would open Gehazi's eyes so that he could see because he was afraid. So, the Lord opened the eyes of Gehazi, and he saw the mountain full of the Lord's horses and chariots of fire all around Elisha. This gave Gehazi insight into the spirit world giving him comfort.

Andrew was trying to figure out the filter dial on the video camera, so he said, "Hey Peter turn the filter dial back and forth.

I think it will show us the transition from the natural world to the spiritual world." So, Peter did that several times. In the **"NATURAL MODE,"** with the filter dial all the way to the left, the camera showed what was really happening as the eye could see. **However, when the filter dial was set all the way to the right, in the "SPIRIT MODE" setting, it gave awareness into the spirit world, viewed from God's perspective, how people are actually known by Jesus.** Andrew said, "Alright, let's try this again, Peter, turn the filter dial to the 'NM' and back to the 'SM.'" As Peter did this several times, the group realized that when in **NM**, the filter meant **'natural mode'** and when in **SM,** it meant **'spiritual mode.'** Then Peter said to Andrew, "Hey, when I turn the filter dial to 'NM' it just stops, but when I turn it to 'SM' it clicks." "Yes!" Andrew said as he snapped his fingers and pointed to Peter. Then Andrew said, "When we are in the Spirit, it's supposed to click."

So, while in the **"SPIRIT MODE"** setting on the camera screen, Brad began to speak, *"Again, the kingdom of heaven is like treasure hidden in a field, which a man found and hid; and for joy over it he goes and sells all that he has and buys that field"* (Matthew 13:44). Then, the camera shut off as if the battery had just died.

Still reeling from all that happened with Lisa, Becky, said to Brad, "Are you kidding me? That's it? What the… I mean, what were you trying to say? What does that even mean?" Brad was speechless, and he looked over to Clark for some adult wisdom and leadership. At that, Jill rolled her eyes back in her head, thinking that her husband wasn't going to know this one either. She walked to the kitchen, asking if anyone wanted a snack? Then Clark looked around at the group, seeing the attentiveness on everyone's face. He said to Jill, "No, I'll pass on the snack. I think I will have to work this one out myself." He was silently praying to Jesus for some help. Then Becky yelled, "Oh my God, look at the scroll! I don't believe it; it just changed. Now it says Matthew 13:44." Clark opened his Bible to that passage and began to read silently, and the kids started to get more anxious as the moments went by. Finally, Clark said, "This chapter of the Bible, the one from Brad's video, is loaded with the parables of Jesus." Then, he led all the kids through the 13th chapter of Matthew (verses 1-52) and the parables that begin with (the kingdom of heaven is like). Afterward, Becky said to Brad and Clark, "Well now I think I have a better understanding of the value of the kingdom of heaven. Anyway, it seems to be high on the list for Jesus to speak about, because he went through seven different situations."

Lisa said to her brother Brad, "Your video was short and sweet. I'm just glad you didn't have to go to hell to prove a point." She ended with a little chuckle, then gave her big brother a hug. Then the video camera powered back up on its own. This time Clark and Jill were on the screen wearing some type of prison uniform. The black and white kind with stripes, having numbers on the left side of their chest. "Hey, what is she saying?" asked Clark. Peter tried to turn up the volume and said, "It won't turn up! It just won't turn up! I don't know what's wrong!"

Discussion Questions:

1) In this chapter, there was a section that dealt with being able to perceive and see into the spirit realm utilizing a passage from II Kings 6:14-18. In the context of your life, what do you think you would see if you saw into the spirit world? Does this thought grip you with fear, or does it bring a sense of wonderment at what may be around you?

2) Is there anything in your life that gives insight into the spirit world? Maybe your Bible or your prayer life. When reading your Bible, do you ever feel like something just clicked? Do you agree with Andrew when he said, "When we are in the Spirit, it's supposed to click?"

3) Looking through Matthew chapter 13, can you locate all of the kingdom parables and the starting place for each one?
Answer: The Sower 3-23, Wheat and Tares 24-30, Mustard Seed 31-32, Leaven 33, Hidden Treasure 44, Pearl of Great Price 45-46, Dragnet 47-50.

Scriptures: II Kings 6:8-18, Matthew 13:44, Matthew 13:1-52.
Discussion Question Scriptures: II Kings 6:14-18, Matthew 13:1-52.

Chapter 6 ~ Saturday

The Church Bulletin

C lark's hand was shaking as he pointed his finger at the camera and said to Peter, "Hey Son, turn up the volume so I can hear what Jill is saying!"

Clark and Jill were still wearing prison uniforms and in the flames of fire and were in the background of the church bulletin photo, the same one that had fallen on the floor earlier. Sara Summers and Senior Pastor James Myers were standing in front of Clark and Jill. It appeared that the Williams's were both burning in hell, screaming out blasphemies, and being in the torment of the flames. Jill was unaware of what was transpiring on the video camera. Then the camera view shifted to Sara and Pastor James. The scene was from the day of the church bulletin photo, where Pastor James took credit for assisting the Summers family with getting into their government-assisted apartment. The instance the camera snapped the photo, pride entered into the Senior Pastor's heart. His depravity and selfishness were winding their way to the surface. Pastor James began to think of all the credit he would receive for helping a poor, down on her luck widow, with four children. Pastor James was guilty of selfish ambitions. "...those who practice such things will not inherit the kingdom of God" (Galatians 5:19-21).

This incident was very similar to what Pastor James did with another family last year when they needed help. Pastor James had no intention of helping them until he discovered there was something in it for himself. They weren't any better off after his assistance, but Pastor James made out very well on his end. He isn't as honest as most people thought.

Sara was seen on the video screen, walking barefoot down a dirt road. She was wearing an old tattered and dirty dress. That road led her to the home of a very prominent businessman in the village. This man had a dinner party one evening, and one of his guests was Jesus. This dusty road left Sara standing outside that man's stone house. Deep sorrow was in her heart as she entered the home of the man who provided the feast. Jesus was sitting at the table when Sara, who was a sinner, walked in. Standing behind Jesus and weeping with a flask of oil in her hands, she began to wash His feet with her tears, and she wiped them with the hairs of her head. Then kissing His feet, she anointed them with the fragrant oil. Now the man who invited Jesus to his house was none-other than Senior Pastor James Myers, within his heart was indignation, and Jesus knew it.

Then Pastor James said to himself, "Well, if Jesus were a prophet, He would have known who this village woman was and that she was a sinner." Then the volume on the camera turned up as Jesus said to him, "James, I have something to say to you." James said, with a slightly cynical undertone, that only Jesus caught. "Alright Sir, go ahead, say what's on your mind." James did not realize that he was talking to the very Man who had the power to save and also the authority to condemn.

Then Jesus said: "There was a certain creditor who had two debtors, one owed five hundred thousand dollars, and the other only fifty. When neither had anything with which to repay, he freely forgave them both. Tell Me James, which of them will love him more?" James answered and said, "I suppose the one whom he forgave the most." Jesus said to him," You have rightly judged." Then He turned to the woman and said to James: "Do you see this woman? I entered your house; you gave Me no water for My feet, but she has washed My feet with her tears and wiped them with the hair of her head. You gave Me no kiss, but this woman has not ceased to kiss My feet since the time I came in. You did not anoint My head with oil, but this woman has anointed My feet with fragrant oil. Therefore, I say to you, her sins are forgiven, for she loved much. But to whom little is forgiven, the same loves little." Then Jesus said to Sara, "Your sins are forgiven." Those at the table with Him began to say to themselves, "Who is this man who even forgives sins?" Then He said to Sara, "Your faith has saved you. Go in peace." (Luke 7:36-50, Ephesians 2:8-10).

The camera zoomed in on the face of the Senior Pastor of the Truth Valley Church. Then Jesus said: "Beware of the false prophets, which come to you in sheep's clothing, but inwardly they are ravening wolves. You will know them by their fruits. Do men gather grapes from thorns or figs from prickly plants? Every good tree provides good fruit, but an immoral tree will only produce immoral fruit. A good tree can't produce immoral fruit; neither can an immoral tree bring forth good fruit. Every tree that does not produce good fruit will be cut down and cast into the fire. You will know them by the fruits that they display in their lives" (Matthew 7:15-20). It was Jesus who had the authority to cast Pastor James into hell. Then the Lord cast Pastor James into the flames of fire. Jesus said, "And the smoke of this man's torment will ascend forever and ever. He will have no rest day nor night; he has worshiped the beast and his image and received the mark of his name" (Revelation 14:11).

Peter was holding the video camera in his hands and began to feel nervous. Clark was looking at him as if Peter were choosing the subject matter that was displayed on the camera screen. Clark began to take it personally that he and Jill had been shown in the flames of the fire, burning in hell. With that nervous feeling taking hold of Peter, his hands became clammy and moist, causing his grip to be unsure. The video camera slipped from his fingers, falling to the floor. Becky sensed that Peter was anxious at seeing his father cast into hell. She noticed that Clark was getting irritated at him. Becky picked up the video camera holding it for all to see, taking the pressure off Peter for the moment.

Discussion Questions:

1) Selfish Ambitions is a work of the flesh from Galatians 5:19-21. Those that practice such things will not inherit the kingdom of God. Review the following scriptures: Romans 2:8-9, Philippians 2:3-4, James 3:14-18. Is there selfishness in your life? If so, how can you remedy this sin and begin to line up with the Spirit of God? One suggestion is to write down the scriptures mentioned here and use them as a guide.

2) Can you think of anywhere in the Bible where selfish ambitions are described? And what were the effects of those actions?

   Answer: Joshua 7:10-26; read all of Joshua chapter 7 for the full account of the impact of selfish ambitions.

Scriptures: Galatians 5:19-21, Luke 7:36-50, Ephesians 2:8-10, Matthew 7:15-20, Revelation 14:11.

Discussion Question Scriptures: Galatians 5:19-21, Romans 2:8-9, Philippians 2:3-4, James 3:14-18, Joshua 7:10-26.

Chapter 7 ~ Saturday

The Rich Man

All was quiet in the cabin as everyone was engrossed in watching the video camera. The scene shifted after Becky picked it up, holding it for Peter after he dropped it.

Jesus began speaking: "There was a certain rich man, who had great wealth and beautiful things all around him, he was clothed in purple and fine linen. This man would celebrate extravagantly every day with great feasts for himself and his friends." As the camera focused on the rich man, it was clear that he was none other than Pastor James. The wealth of James was so excessive that a typical meal consisted of three turkeys, five whole chickens, and more steaks than anyone could count. They were stacked four or five high on platters and arranged in rows. There were countless side dishes and numerous desserts and pastries. This type of meal was standard for James and his friends. He had thirty to forty servants preparing his meals every day. This particular meal was an everyday dinner. The excess was thrown out, as none of the servants were ever permitted to eat any of the leftovers. James was not very hungry that day because he had eaten a large lunch.

A certain beggar named Lazarus, who was laid at the gate of James every day, was full of sores all over his body. Day by day, the poor beggar Lazarus endured watching all the food that James counted as waste be tossed into the fire. James had guards that would ensure the servants disposed of all the leftover food in the fire. There was not even a kernel of corn that was given to feed the poor. This poor beggar had only one desire, and that was to receive just a few of the scraps that fell from James's table. He wasn't asking for much; a piece of bread would satisfy his deep hunger. As this poor beggar lay at the gate of James's mansion, the dogs would come and lick his wounds and sores. It seemed as if the dogs were the only ones that had any compassion for this poor beggar

Then one day, as James was on his way to town, as he often did, he stepped over the beggar man lying at his gate. However, James noticed that he had died during the night. Without any hesitation, James continued to town to buy some more food for an upcoming feast. The spirit of Lazarus was carried by the angels to paradise to be in the presence of Abraham. However, his emaciated body was not given a proper burial.

While James was buying items for his upcoming feast in town, he was bitten by a poisonous viper and died within the hour. A great cry sounded, and it was made known that a noble man had died. Hundreds and even thousands attended his funeral. He was laid in a grand mausoleum, half the size of his mansion. James's family held his funeral service for five days and set a seventy-day mourning period for the entire country to grieve his death.

It came to pass when James opened his eyes, he found himself in Hades–the realm of the dead and being in torment. He was able to see Abraham, who was far away, with Lazarus being comforted, resting by his side. James being in great anguish, cried, "Father Abraham, have mercy on me. Send Lazarus, that he may dip the tip of his finger in water, and cool my tongue, for I am being tormented and tortured in this flame of fire." But Abraham said, "Son, remember in your lifetime you received wealth and luxury whereas Lazarus was lowly and poor having nothing of his own and never had enough food to eat. But now he is comforted, and you are in your torment of fire burning night and day." Then Abraham said to James, as the flames began to overtake him, "There's a deep gorge fixed between us that makes it impossible for me to go to you, and consequently, you cannot come to me." As James thought on this last statement, he pleaded, "I beg you, father Abraham, send Lazarus to my brother who has never believed in Jesus Christ. Please send him to testify of Jesus, so my brother Chris may avoid this place of eternal torment." Abraham said to him, "He has Moses and the prophets; let him read and hear what they have written." James replied, "No father Abraham, he will only repent and seek God's righteousness if someone returns from the dead and speaks to him." Then Abraham replied, "If he will not hear Moses, the prophets, and the gospel, neither will he be persuaded if someone rose from the dead" (Luke 16:19-31).

Pastor James had not served the Lord Jesus Christ but was instead a self-serving man and had never repented of his sin nature. Those in the room watched in horror as they observed their very own senior pastor vanish in the flames of fire. He was belting out words of blasphemies, which were very similar to that of Lisa earlier but with a more depraved nature. Abraham had nothing left to say to James (James 3:1).

The camera panned out of that scene. Then Jesus said: "As my friend Abraham said, 'They have Moses, the prophets, and all of the Bible.' Hear and read what I have said. (Psalms 40:7, Luke 24:44). Come to Me, all you who labor and are heavy laden, and I will give you rest. Take My yoke upon you and learn from Me, for I am gentle and lowly in heart, and you will find rest for your souls. For My yoke is easy, and My burden is light" (Matthew 11:28-30). Then Jesus turned and looked directly into the camera and said, "Remember the rich man burning in the flames of the fire, being in torments. He has been there for over two thousand years. That's two thousand years of suffering night and day, with eternity ahead of him. All because he never turned to Me and repented of his sinful ways. Seek Me, and you will find Me!" (Jeremiah 29:13).

At that, Peter was exceedingly shaken. He headed outside to weep, as it was his own father who was destined for hell if he couldn't find his way to repentance. (II Corinthians 7:10, Luke 7:36-39).

Mark seeing his best friend upset, followed him outside and tried to console him. It was evident why Peter's dad had been acting so odd lately. After Peter regained his composure, he asked his best friend Mark point-blank, "Mark, have you ever turned your life over to Jesus Christ and repented of your sin, not letting pride rule you like my father has?" Mark looked at Peter, unable to find any words to respond to that question. He lowered his head and looked at the ground, saying nothing as silence filled the night air (I Kings 18:21).

Discussion Questions:
1) Multiple Choice: pick the most appropriate answer that fits your life's desires as applied to your eternal soul. Given my current life situation, I see myself as spending my eternal existence in the following manner:
   a) In the presence of Jesus Christ in His Father's kingdom (John 14:1-4).
   b) Being in torments of fire and brimstone in the presence of the holy angels and the Lamb like the rich man (Revelation 14:10-11).
   c) Being in torments in Hades in the flame (Luke 16:23-24).
   d) None of the above: I chose to ignore that hell or the Lake of fire existed, even though the Bible and Jesus speak of them both.
2) How would you answer the question from this chapter that Peter asked Mark? "Have you ever turned your life over to Jesus Christ and repented of your sin, not letting pride rule you like my father has?"
3) Have you ever been so tired that you didn't know what to do with yourself while lying on your bed, not being able to fall asleep? How would it be in hell or the lake of fire for eternity where they have no rest day nor night? (Revelation 14:11). Think of yourself being in a place where you are denied rest day and night forever. Then secondly, add the smoke of your

torment ascending forever and ever. Take a few minutes to think about that scenario. Now contemplate the following from I Kings 18:21. When you do not say a word, you are, by default, denying the Lord that bought you with His blood. That was the case in this chapter when Mark put his head down and looked at the ground, saying nothing. (Acts 20:28 & Ephesians 1:14).

Scriptures: Luke 16:19-31, James 3:1, Psalms 40:7, Luke 24:44, Matthew 11:28-30, Jeremiah 29:13, II Corinthians 7:10, Luke 7:36-39, I Kings 18:21.

Discussion Question Scriptures: John 14:1-4, Revelation 14:10-11, Luke 16:23-24, Revelation 14:11, I Kings 18:21, Acts 20:28, Ephesians 1:14.

Chapter 8 ~ Saturday

Will God Grant them Repentance

When Peter and Mark went outside, the video camera came back on by itself. "Hey, what's she saying," Clark asked Becky. The group was watching the scene of the Williams's burning in the flames of hell, each wearing a prison uniform. Becky tried to turn up the volume, then she said, "It won't turn up! I don't know how to make it work! I just don't know what's wrong with it!" Then, the camera volume turned up on its own. Jill walked in and saw in horror what was transpiring before everyone's eyes. The Williams's were howling out screams filled with blasphemies towards God that sounded so gruesome that everyone had to turn away. At that, Becky ran outside, and her best friend Brenda followed her. As she did, Becky handed the camera to Lisa.

Having regained his composure, after seeing his father portrayed as the rich man, Peter decided that he was ready to go back inside. While walking outside, Becky and Brenda passed Peter and Mark, who were on their way back to the cabin.

As the Williams's were burning in the flames of hell, the camera scene transitioned to a beautiful Sunday morning. Jill and Clark were sitting at a corner nook table in the Coffee Barn at Truth Valley Church with another couple. Two of the Summers children were at a table behind them as Jill was talking to the other couple. Jill said, "You know, I haven't seen Sara lately, it seems as though she has become quite the little backslider since her husband passed away." The other couple hadn't given it any thought until Jill put it into their mind. However, Clark, in keeping the peace, said nothing. Then it became known at Truth Valley that Sara Summers was a backslider, among other things, such as keeping late hours. Someone even said that they saw her walking away from the Skeleton Crew Pub and Eatery with a couple of men of the drinking sort.

Lisa became disgusted at what she was watching, stood up while still holding the video camera, and handed it to Peter, who had just come back into the cabin. Lisa went over to the kitchen table to sit alone. Peter, having the video camera again, sat down and held it for all to see.

The camera scene continued. Walking away from the pub, that part was partially true. The implication of walking away from the pub was that Sara spent time backsliding in the pub with men who were drinking. What actually happened that day was quite different.

Sara had a friend from work, Zackery Kelley, who had recently lost his wife to an illness. She stopped off at the Little Red Rose Bud Flower Shop to get him some flowers as a pick me up. On the way out of the flower shop, Sara walked past the Skeleton Crew Pub and Eatery. On her way to her car, two men walked out of the pub. It had been raining that afternoon, and Sara could not get a parking space close to the flower shop. She gave the flowers to her friend, and it cheered him up a bit that someone cared enough to take a few minutes out of their day to bring him some flowers. So, it was recorded in heaven that Sara purchased some flowers for a friend and walked by a pub where two men were exiting. She continued to her car without incident. But it went down a little different at the church Coffee

Barn. Then Jill added, "Bless her little heart for trying so hard." Well, that's the talk of the church at the Coffee Barn, where the gossip goes down, and the truth is never found (Romans 1:28-32).

The Williams's were once again seen burning in hell on the camera screen. Now the works of the flesh are evident, just as I also told you in time past, that those who practice such things will not inherit the kingdom of God (Galatians 5:19-21). Hypocrites! Well did Isaiah prophesy about you, saying: These people draw near to Me with their mouth and honor Me with their lips, but their heart is far from Me. And in vain, they worship Me, teaching as doctrines the commandments of men (Matthew 15:7-9).

Then the Williams's were seen in the Truth Valley Church sanctuary worshiping God with their lips, while their hearts were far from Him (Matthew 15:7-11). Then an angel spoke directly to the Williams's with this warning. You shall love the Lord your God with all your heart, with all your soul, and with all your mind. This is the first and great commandment. And the second one is like it, you shall love your neighbor as you would yourself. On these two commandments hang all the law and the prophets (Matthew 22:37-40). And a servant of the Lord must not quarrel but be gentle to all, able to teach, patient, in humility correcting those who are in opposition, if God perhaps will grant them repentance, so that they may know the truth, and that they may come to their senses and escape the snare of the devil, having been taken captive by him to do his will (II Timothy 2:24-26). The sacrifices of God are a broken spirit, a broken and a contrite heart—These, O God, You will not despise [KJV] (Psalms 51:17). Then the Angel departed, leaving Clark and Jill burning in hell on the camera screen. Their screams filled the atmosphere at the Cabin in the Way.

Peter was still holding the video camera with the Williams's burning in the flame. Clark said, "Alright, Peter, I think we have seen enough; you can turn that thing off now." Peter said to Clark, "That's the problem, I can't turn it off, I just can't!" Jill

39

was getting frustrated and began to berate Peter, demanding that he immediately turn off the video camera. She and Clark continued to be in the flames of hell on the camera screen, and their screams filled the air. "It won't turn off, I've tried, I've tried everything," Peter said. Then Jill grabbed the video camera out of Peter's hands and threw it to the floor, smashing it into a hundred pieces. Then there was silence in the cabin. After that, Jill walked outside. She walked past Becky and Brenda, who were sitting on the stone wall in front of the cabin. They appeared to be praying but paused for a moment to look at Jill, who was passing by. Jill said to them, rather snippily, "So, what are you two looking at anyway?" Then she headed down the second marked trail.

Becky was upset earlier at seeing the Williams's in the flames of hell, so she needed to go outside to get some fresh air. Brenda followed her and began talking with her. After Jill walked past them, Brenda said to Becky, "I think it's time we go back inside to see how the others are doing." Both girls walked back into the cabin as Becky wiped the tears from her face, seeming somewhat humbled. As the girls entered the cabin, they could see that everyone was shaken up. They stepped over all the broken pieces of the video camera. They saw that all the other students had gathered around their youth leader Clark and were all praying with him.

Discussion Questions:
1) According to the Apostle Paul, gossip is a work of the flesh. Do you agree that it is justly an offense that would preclude someone from entering into the kingdom of God? If you disagree, then how do you interpret Galatians 5:19-21?
2) Are there teachings, known as doctrines, that are actually commandments of men?
   Answer: Matthew 15:1-20.
3) Do you think Jill was justified when she destroyed the video camera seeing that Peter was unable to turn it off? Would you like to expand on your answer?

4) According to II Timothy 2:24-26: Is it possible that you are being held captive by the devil, doing his will? If so, the only remedy to escape the trap of the god of this world is through the Spirit of truth that proceeds from the Father in Heaven, the Holy Spirit.

Scriptures: Romans 1:28-32, Galatians 5:19-21, Matthew 15:7-11, Matthew 22:37-40, II Timothy 2:24-26, Psalms 51:17.

Note: Read Romans 1:28-32 in the Amplified Version.

Discussion Question Scriptures: Galatians 5:19-21, Matthew 15:1-20, II Timothy 2:24-26.

Chapter 9 ~ Sunday

Hasn't it Caused Enough Trouble

Sunday morning came quickly for the campers as the sun began to rise over the mountains. Clark lived up to his part of the bargain, making the coffee and starting the pancakes on the griddle. The bacon was sizzling in the skillet sending out a sweet aroma blending perfectly with the crisp mountain air at the Cabin in the Way. Clark walked over to the boy's side of the cabin and roused all of the guys, reminding them that they also had to help make breakfast. They were the ones who came up short on the fundraising drive; however, it wasn't for the lack of trying. The girls manage to squeak by with an $18.96 victory. Thus, giving them an extra thirty minutes of sleep, which they took full advantage of that morning.

Somehow Clark convinced the boys to get out of their warm beds. That morning was unusually cold, and the late autumn frost had blanketed the ground. "Hey, Brad and Andrew, do you guys want to stoke the wood-burning stove? It's a little chilly in here," said Clark. The fire had died down to just a few coals. Brad and

Andrew thought this was the perfect opportunity to get out of making breakfast. They were on their assigned task without any hesitation; besides, they were getting pretty cold themselves. What a motivator providing for yourself can be, especially when it's your flesh and not the Holy Spirit driving you.

Peter and Mark dragged themselves out of their warm double quilts, slowly making their way to the table. It was Mark who first noticed that the video camera was back together, sitting on the corner of the kitchen table, without even a scratch. Brad and Andrew each grabbed an armful of firewood from the front porch, but they didn't notice the hooded man with his face concealed, vanishing into the deep dark woods.

Peter grabbed the video camera and put it under his pillow. While he sat on his bed, he remembered the discussion just moments ago when Mark whispered to him, "Hey Peter, the video camera is sitting on the table, hurry up and put it away. Hasn't it caused enough trouble already?!" Peter didn't know what time it was when Jill made it back to the cabin after she walked out in a huff the night before. He felt somewhat responsible for all that had happened since that first encounter with those hooded men.

With a frying pan in one hand and a coffee pot in the other, Clark said to Mark, while Peter was still putting away the video camera, "Thanks, Mark, for cleaning up that mess. I stepped on the broken camera pieces while I was getting the coffee going this morning." Mark realized at that moment that the video camera had become new again between the time that Clark made the coffee and when he and Peter got out of their beds. Once again, Mark knew that the truth was not going to be easy to explain, so he just pretended like he didn't hear anything that Clark said to him. As Peter walked into the kitchen, Clark said, "Peter, get out the eggs, butter, plates, silverware, and flip those pancakes over there on the griddle. Oh, and please," he added. Peter speedily went to work, helping with breakfast, trying to forget everything to do with that video camera.

With the cabin now warm and cozy, the girls begin to rise for the day. They were hungry as ever, since dinner the night before was mainly snacks. Everyone had been a little distracted from the events that transpired on the video camera and the ones that took place in real life, at the Cabin in the Way. Lisa was the first of the girls to the kitchen table with her sweatshirt, sweat pants, and fuzzy slippers. Regarding their younger sister Lisa, Daisy said to Brenda, "She seems more at peace after she repented yesterday. Don't you think so?" Without answering her, Brenda walked over and sat next to Lisa, embracing her while both girls had tears of joy streaming down their faces. Daisy joined her two sisters, making it a group hug. Becky plopped herself down with the three other girls joining them. Being an only child, Becky had adopted herself into the Summers family.

Breakfast went as planned. Almost all the food was consumed by the hungry teenagers. They devoured their feast like a bunch of fishermen rescued after a month on the high seas without any chow. All the kids contributed to clean up duty, so they could begin their hike to the Edwardsville Mine and Millworks Company for their tour of the abandoned facility. This was the highlight of every trip to The Cabin in the Deep Dark Woods. Clark made a plate of food and covered it with foil. As the kids finished the last few dishes, they could hear him say to Jill, "I made you a plate of breakfast. Are you going to get up and go to the mine with the rest of us this morning?" Jill just rolled over in bed, without saying a word.

Andrew had prepared another message as the group began to gather back around the kitchen table. Lisa, still wearing her fuzzy slippers, was the first one to the table, Becky followed, with her Bible tucked under her arm. All the teenagers were sitting and listening attentively, being rather humbled by the previous night's events. There was silence for a few moments until Andrew opened up his Bible and said, "Today I'm going to be reading from II Timothy 2:15. Here the Apostle Paul said, 'Be diligent to present yourself approved to God, a worker who does not need to be ashamed, rightly dividing the word of truth.'" Andrew went on to say, "In this verse, we see two elements. The first is a commission to get involved in studying God's written word. And the second is to let God, through the Holy Spirit, reveal that word to your heart. Revealing what in your life is of God and what is not of His nature."

Andrew continued with his message as everyone listened attentively. Even Jill listened from her bed. As he finished, Andrew said: "Salvation is so important, each believer must spend time in God's word to ensure, based upon the Bible, whether they are truly saved or just living a lie. It would be better to find out beforehand if you were living in a false hope of salvation, by studying the scriptures, rather than having Jesus say to you on judgment day, 'depart from Me!'" Andrew looked at the group, and with a long pause, while he made eye contact with everyone sitting at the table he said, "You choose, when is the best time to find out the truth about you?" With that last statement, Becky began to look deep within herself, and she was the last one to leave the table that morning.

See Appendix C for the entirety of Salvation, a Measurable Objective.

Soon after, the campers were ready to head out the door. Their gear was set for the hike to the Edwardsville Mine and Millworks Company. Everyone was gathered in front of the cabin by the stone wall to begin their hike. Then Peter darted back into the cabin to retrieve the video camera and stuffed it into his backpack. As he headed back outside, he saw Jill in the kitchen scarfing down a pancake and a piece of bacon with a half a cup of coffee in her other hand. Stopping, he asked her, "Mrs. Williams, are you coming to the mine with all of us this morning?" Jill knew she had been looking forward to the mine tour, as she was a secret history buff in her own right. She said, "Yes, Peter, tell Clark I'll be just a couple minutes more."

Discussion Questions:
1) Do you know anyone like Mark that can't seem to tell the truth? What advice would you give to Mark in this chapter when he pretended not to hear anything that Clark said to him?
2) Brenda and Daisy seemed to notice a difference in their younger sister Lisa the morning after she repented and asked God to be a part of her life. Can you remember a time, if there was a time, when there was a change in your life?

3) Depart from Me: You choose; when is the best time to know the truth about yourself? What is the truth about you? Are you living with a false hope of salvation? What will Jesus say to you after you pass from this life?

Scriptures: II Timothy 2:15.

Discussion Question Scriptures: none.

Chapter 10 ~ Sunday

The Ranger Station

The youth group was on their way to the Edwardsville Ranger Station for their tour of the mine and millworks company. Brad explained various items along the way since the hike was going to take about twenty minutes. Brad continued by saying, "Hey guys, did you know the cabin that we are staying in was originally intended to be a church?" "I had no idea," said Lisa. Brad said, "The Pastor died before it was finished. Years later, the townspeople completed it and turned it into a one-room schoolhouse called the School in the Way. Do you see that red covered bridge up ahead? It was built so the children from the miners' village could attend the school." "You did your homework," said Andrew. Brad did his best to conceal a grin. Then he said, "Hey guys, look over there," as he pointed out some discarded rock piles that were from an era gone by, from the abandoned mining operation.

As the group approached the ranger station, which was built on the mine and millworks property, Brad pointed out one of the adits. He explained that the adits were the entrance to the mine tunnel, which is appropriately called a drift and driven into the side of the mountain. As the group passed the adit, Brad pointed out that its opening had been gated by the parks department many years ago. Soon they arrived at the ranger station and met their tour guide, Ranger Jim Arnett. As he greeted them, Mark whispered into Peter's ear, "Hey, I'm sure glad you left the video camera back at the cabin."

Jill handed Ranger Jim the reservation paperwork, and he officially checked them in. Then the group was escorted to the classroom. Ranger Jim said, "I'm going to tell you about the history of the Edwardsville Mine and Millworks Company, the School in the Way, and the Cabin in the Way." During this time, everyone started to acquire knowledge of the people that lived there long ago. Ranger Jim pointed to a memorial plaque hanging on the wall in honor of the late Pastor Daniel Edwards, for which the town was also named after. He began to read it for all to hear:

> My dearest Lord and Heavenly Father, this day, I
> beckon unto You my solemn thoughts and prayer. On
> this very ground, I kneel before You in all reverence.
> I ask that You bless this land and cabin and that You
> pour out Your Spirit on the hearts of all that enter
> through the narrow gate and that You keep them in
> 'the Way' of the saints who walked before them,
> Amen.

Ranger Jim said to the group: "This was the prayer of a man named Daniel Edwards. He had a deep conviction to the will of God; he prayed this prayer before starting to build his church. It is now the cabin that you are staying in this weekend, but you guys call it the Cabin in the Deep Dark Woods." Ranger Jim went on to explain the in "the Way" part of the name saying: "You see, Pastor Edwards had called it the Church in the Way, signifying the way of the saints (Acts 9:1-2). And so, it stuck, thus becoming what it is today, the Cabin in the Way. I can attest to the value of that man's prayer and that his prayer did make its way to the throne of grace (Hebrews 4:16). You see, my great—grandfather's name was Blake Arnett, and it was Daniel Edwards's prayer that shaped the life of that young boy, transforming him into the man of God that he became. Blake's parents, who were from the mining village, were not believers in God. They believed that there was a God, but they never cared enough to search for God's truth. That was until Blake became curious while he was attending the School in the Way. During prayer time one morning, Blake asked his teacher who the Holy Spirit was. These are the three questions that Blake asked her."

What is the Holy Spirit? How can we get the Holy Spirit? And what does the Holy Spirit do for us?

Ranger Jim said: "This is what Blakes's teacher had to say. 'The Holy Spirit is that Spirit sent by Jesus to guide us into all truth (John 14:15-18). The Holy Spirit is poured out on the hearts of all who want to be led by God. You receive the Holy Spirit by being broken and humble or even as some by becoming like a child. (Mark 10:14-16, Psalms 51:17, Acts 2:1-47). It depends on where someone is when they feel the need for God in their life. The Holy Spirit will write the ways of Jesus on our hearts so that we stay on the right path. (Hebrews 10:16-17, II Corinthians 3:2-3). It is God's truth that comes from the Holy Spirit that will keep us in God's ways. Whenever someone begins to steer away from the narrow path, the Holy Spirit will convict them. This brings us back into agreement with God if we yield to His voice'" (Hebrews 4:11-13).

Then Ranger Jim said: "After that answer from his teacher, Blake began his life long walk with Jesus. It not only changed his life, but it also changed the lives of his mother and father, and it also changed and affected the generations that followed."

Ranger Jim informed the group that he would accompany them to the main adit, where they would begin their tour of the mine. As everyone left the classroom, they were issued a helmet and a headlamp. Along the way to the entrance to the mine, Ranger Jim pointed out various items around the mine and mill works property. There were some rather large discarded rock piles and an abandoned and almost fallen down dormitory and office building. Once the group arrived at the adit, Ranger Jim unlocked the chained iron gate and said, "I hope at least one of you youngsters brought a video camera along with you. You won't want to miss any of the action that's going to happen inside this mine today." And with a slight grin, he looked over at Peter and gave him a wink. At that, a little smile came on Ranger Jim's face as the padlock and chain fell to the ground.

Discussion Questions:

1) Do you know anyone that believes that there is a God but does not care enough to search for God's truths? Could this person be you?

2) Can you answer the three questions that Blake asked his teacher in this chapter? The answers are contained in the passage [This is what Blakes's teacher had to say].
   a) What is the Holy Spirit?
   b) How can we get the Holy Spirit?
   c) And what does the Holy Spirit do for us?

3) What scriptures represent Jesus as a way to salvation?
   Answer: John 10:7-9, John 14:6, Ephesians 2:14-18, and Hebrews 10:19-25.

4) In Genesis 3:6, Eve saw the fruit, she touched the fruit, and then she ate it. Compare that with Mark 4:3-20, we hear the word, the word touches our heart, and then we feed on the word. How has your life been affected by Mark 4:3-20? Remember, the word is the Word from John 1:1-5.

Scriptures: Acts 9:1-2, Hebrews 4:16, John 14:15-18, Mark 10:14-16, Psalms 51:17, Acts 2:1-47, Hebrews 10:16-17, II Corinthians 3:2-3, Hebrews 4:11-13.

Discussion Question Scriptures: John 10:7-9, John 14:6, Ephesians 2:14-18, Hebrews 10:19-25, Genesis 3:6, Mark 4:3-20, John 1:1-5.

Chapter 11 ~ Sunday

A Psalm of Repentance

A ssociate Pastor Arron Carpenter addressed the Truth Valley Church from the pulpit by saying, "Blessed are the poor in spirit." He was filling in for Pastor James, who had taken ill. Pastor Carpenter said, "Today's message is from Psalms 51, and it is in this passage that true repentance is found in the first 17 verses."

Pastor Arron Carpenter's message: The Psalmist David asked God for mercy, desiring to be cleansed from his iniquities and sins. He acknowledged his transgressions before the Lord, stating that he had sinned against the Lord, and the Lord knew it. David brought out that God longs for truth in the inward parts and that in the hidden part of a man or woman, God will make known His wisdom. He further highlights the desire to be purged, cleaned, and washed, with faith following giving place for purity. We also see a desire to have joy and gladness. David wanted God to hide His face from all of the sins of his heart. Only God can create a clean heart and a perfect spirit in a man or woman. His desire was to stay in the Lord's presence as there is nothing else that can compare. There was a great desire to have the joy of salvation with an emphasis on joy. Joy is also a fruit of the spirit.

Through faith, the Lord provided David all the desires of his heart. As long as they are rooted and grounded in the will of God.

David goes on in faith to express that when these points are established that he will share the message of God to others, and he would teach them the ways of God. There's also a deep faith that sinners and unbelievers will be converted. There's a desire to be delivered from not only the sin but also the guilt of the sin. When this deliverance was granted, the author said he would sing of the righteousness of God. There is a praise to God that is found through faith. It's clear that God does not want religious declarations; instead, He delights in a broken spirit and a contrite heart; these are God's delights. To enter into salvation, it must be understood that one of the first steps is to seek repentance from the Lord. This was made very clear in Mark 1:14-15, as Jesus said to repent and believe in the gospel.

Carpenter continued with his message explaining to the congregation the need to be born again (John 3:1-21). He made the statement that Jesus was clear that to enter the kingdom of God, a man or woman must be born again. As he concluded his sermon, he further emphasized the need for holiness, reading from I Peter 1:16. The Choir began to sing, and an invitation was given for all who desired to be filled with the Holy Spirit. Many came forward that morning desiring to be born again, filled with the Holy Spirit, and baptized in the name of Jesus. As church ended, those individuals desiring to be led by God were encouraged to join a home Bible study where they could be mentored in small group settings. It was John the Baptist who prepared the Way for the ministry of Jesus. In these small group studies, the Way of Jesus will be grounded in the hearts of the individuals desiring to be led by God.

Discussion Question:

1) Although it is the most famous scripture, John 3:16 is timeless. Have you read it lately? For God so loved the world, that he gave his only begotten Son, that whosoever believeth in him should not perish, but have everlasting life. [KJV]

Scriptures: Psalms 51:1-17, Mark 1:14-15, John 3:1-21, I Peter 1:16.

Discussion Question Scriptures: none.

Chapter 12 ~ Sunday

Words of Tears

After Ranger Jim unlocked the chained iron gate, he guided the adults and teens through the main adit into the drift. Everyone was amazed at the scenery inside the mine. Ranger Jim explained what they were looking at as they made their way deeper into the mine. Brad pointed out the heavy timbers that the miners had put in place to shore up the drifts so long ago. "Wow, this is incredible," Becky said to Daisy. Both girls were looking at the various items illuminated by the beam of light from their headlamps.

Everyone was preoccupied with the scenery inside the mine. Then Ranger Jim whispered to Peter, "Hey Son, does that video camera have the **'PM'** feature on it, you know the **'projector mode'** model? If it does, it will work great down here in the mine." Peter was speechless and shocked that the ranger had the slightest inclination he had a video camera in his possession. He thought to himself, "What did he mean 'projector mode'?" Peter once again fell behind the rest of the group. He was no longer thinking about the mine but was fixated on finding the "projector mode" feature on the camera. So, when no one was looking, Peter kneeled as he sat his backpack down and pulled out the video camera. Suddenly, a hand grabbed his arm sharply. Peter looked up and saw his best friend Mark looking down at him with a glaring stare. "Dude, I thought you left that video camera back at the cabin," Mark said as he seemed to be peering into Peter's very soul. Then he added, "You're going to get us in all kinds of trouble down here. You need to put that thing away." Peter looked up at Mark and said, "It's too late!" Mark asked, "It's too late for what? What are you talking about, Peter? It's too late for …" Just then, Mark figured it out as the video camera had powered on by itself. Peter informed Mark that there was a new feature on the camera. Mark was speechless as the video camera shined a beam of light on the mine wall. Peter had already switched the filter dial to **"PM" for Projector Mode**, turning the video camera into a movie projector.

There on the mine wall, for all to see, was Becky sitting in the senior pastor's office. This scene was taking place at the Truth Valley Church. It was like she was waiting for a meeting to begin. This gained the attention of everyone as the projector was putting out a bright beam of light.

The group observed the scene unfolding on the mine wall. Then Peter explained the setting because he recognized that it was taking place in his father's church office. The scene on the mine wall showed Becky sitting in a chair, facing away from the door. A woman came up behind her and placed her hands on Becky's shoulders. Then Becky looked up and saw in a mirror an older woman who appeared to be about fifty years of age standing behind her. Then this woman began to prophesy over Becky. The older woman who appeared to be Becky's older self, began to speak prophetically, saying to her younger self with a sorrowful tone that only comes from deep within the spirit: "The rededication and commitment that you made during this trip while sitting outside with Brenda on the stone wall last night was not your salvation. Although you made this commitment with tears, it was not true repentance. You still hold in your heart, bitterness, strife, and wickedness. Since you have refused the Holy Spirit's entrance into your life, you will need to press into the kingdom of God and let the Lord Jesus Christ clothe you with His righteousness. Your main problem, Becky, is you seek your own righteousness and not the righteousness of Christ the Lord. You will walk through dry places, happiness and contentment will be far from you until godly sorrow comes upon your life. This is the Lords doing, and it is beautiful in His sight."

Then the older woman handed the younger woman a book of all the words prophesied over her, and the younger woman ate the book. The younger woman began to weep inconsolably as the words of the prophecy began to flow as words like tears washing over her. The older woman began speaking once again but was not heard. The younger woman was still weeping words like tears when the older woman's voice was heard as if she knew who was watching that scene unfolding on the mine wall. She looked directly into the camera and said, "God loves Becky so much that He will spare nothing to get her attention as she walks in darkness, holding to the lies of the false prophets who say, 'Peace, peace! When there is no peace,'" (Jeremiah 6:14).

Then the video camera shut off on its own, and it was dark in the mine again. Everyone, including Ranger Jim, had turned off their headlamps. As Becky stood in the darkness, it felt to her like hours before someone turned on a headlamp. She felt a deep shock, which made her feel overwhelmed to the point of falling to her knees. All at once, the headlamps came back on. There on her knees, Becky began to weep, and the girls consoled her. Clark looked at Peter and Mark and said sternly, "I thought we were done with that thing!" Jill was more shocked than anyone because she knew she had destroyed the video camera the night before.

Discussion Questions:
1) Have you ever had an experience of praying in deep sorrow that only comes from within the spirit like was portrayed with Becky's older self? If so, how long ago, and if not, is this something that you desire?

2) Do you think someone can have a false hope of salvation? What is your opinion of saying the sinner's prayer?

3) Multiple Choice: If a loved one were to say the sinner's prayer, what are some elements that should be included in their prayer?

    a) Just repeating someone's else words.

    b) Elements along the same line, as found in Psalms 51:1-17.

    c) Being alone and coming to the end of themselves, then asking God into their heart to lead and guide them as their personal Savior.

    d) None of the above, as I don't hold to the sinner's prayer.

Scriptures: Jeremiah 6:14

Discussion Question Scriptures: Psalms 51:1-17.

Chapter 13 ~ Sunday

The Vault

Ranger Jim leaned over and whispered in Peter's ear, "Son, did you find the **'Repentance Mode' feature yet?"** Adding with emphasis, by twisting his hand all the way to the right, saying, "Look for the **'RM'** on the filter dial." Then, he gave Peter another wink and patted him on the shoulder, making his way down the drift deeper into the mine. Ranger Jim explained the various aspects of the mine to the group saying, "Now look over here, and you can see along the wall where the miners used their picks to dig out the mountain." He ran his hand along the wall, getting the attention of the group.

This gave Peter some breathing room to look for the **"RM"** feature on the filter dial. Then, Mark grabbed the video camera out of Peter's hands. As he did, he heard Lisa ask Ranger Jim what kind of mine it was. That gave Mark enough time to put the video camera in his own backpack, avoiding any more trouble. Ranger Jim answered her, "Lisa, this was an iron ore mine; well, mostly iron ore." Then he added a little humor, "I've found a few nickels over the years." He said that to give Mark a bit more time, they all began to laugh at the ranger's corny little joke. By then, Mark had finished tucking the camera into his backpack. Then the group made their way into the

"VAULT" area. That's what they called it at the Edwardsville Mine and Millworks Company.

Everyone was in awe of the vaulted ceiling with its nine to almost ten-foot height. Which was grand compared to the drifts that were no more than six feet high. Ranger Jim began to explain that the vault had an abundance of iron ore, which was why the ceiling was so high. As he was finishing his speech on the vault area, there was a bright light coming from Mark's backpack and a lot of ruckus. Clark asked, "Mark, what's going on with your backpack?" Mark said, "Oh no, oh no, I put the video camera in there!"

Andrew's voice shouted from Mark's backpack, "I'm going to kill you! I'm going to kill you as soon as I can stomp you!" In the background, things were heard falling to the ground. As this violent scene unfolded from Mark's backpack, Clark finally said, "Mark, go ahead and take that thing out so everyone can see what's happening." Mark quickly placed his backpack on the ground so he could access the video camera. *Everyone could hear Andrew's voice scream, "You're not going to get away from me! I've got you now! Get ready to face your death you little piece of slime!"* After that, Mark held the video camera, and it was still in the **'projector mode.'** Then everyone turned off their headlamps.

As they watched, the camera projected a beam of light on the giant wall in the vault area. The mine was once again lit up due to the light beam flowing from the video camera. The scene unfolded with Andrew, who was very relaxed, picking up his clipboard and a broom and shovel that had fallen during the commotion, just moments ago. He calmly placed them neatly back into the corner. Andrew appeared to be about thirty years old in this scene. Then a young man walked in and said to Andrew, "Good morning boss, I'm here to help you with inventory today. Is everything alright? I heard a lot of yelling and banging as I walked in." Andrew said, "Oh, yes, everything is fine now. I just hate cockroaches. Not to worry, though, I just killed that slimy creepy-crawly as you were walking in."

The camera panned around, showing that these two men were working in a vast warehouse with countless racks that required the use of forklifts to access the stock. Without looking up from his clipboard, Andrew said to the young man, "Hey, what's your name, their buddy? How did you get through personnel without being issued a name tag?" The man replied, "My mother calls me Stephen." Andrew said, "Yes, Stephen, you are here to help me with inventory today." Stephen looked around at the warehouse's enormous size and said, "Wow, that sure is a lot of stuff to go through in one day." Andrew sensed that Stephen was not clear on exactly what they were going to inventory. Putting his clipboard down for a moment, he said to him, "Stephen, we're going to inventory the three items in the vault right behind me." Picking up his clipboard, Andrew gestured to a walk-in sized vault behind him, like you would see in a bank.

Stephen asked, "What's that noise in the background?" Andrew said, "Oh, you mean that song?" "Yes," Stephen said, adding, "I've never heard that song before." Andrew said, "Why that's 'The Old Rugged Cross,' I always play it whenever I inventory the vault. Just listen to the lyrics." The men paused to listen for a moment.

Andrew continued, "The old rugged cross is one of the items we will be inventorying today." Again, Andrew gestured to the vault." Relieved, Stephen said, "Okay, we are just inventorying the vault today." Andrew answered: "That's right, Stephen, and just the three items stored in it. Those three items are essential. They are the Cross of Jesus, the Veil that was torn, and the Testimony of the New Covenant." Stephen said, "Okay, boss, but I must warn you, I've never heard of any those items before." "WHAT?!" Andrew declared sharply, even surprising himself. He took a deep breath before he spoke again, then said, "You have never heard of the Cross of Jesus, the Veil that was torn, and the Testimony of the New Covenant?" Stephen said, rather innocently, "No, I've never heard about any of them before. Oh, and who is this Jesus fella that you are talking about?" Andrew was in the midst of a perplexing situation, scratching his head, somewhat speechless.

"Okay, okay, okay," Andrew said, in such a low tone that Stephen could hardly hear him. Andrew was stalling as he was processing where to even begin, and then he said, "Let's start by opening the vault." Andrew opened the combination lock by pressing the keypad code 5-6-4-6-3-1-6, then the vault door opened. Stephen was impressed that Andrew pressed such an extended code by memory. Andrew told him the code was derived from the Bible verse, John 3:16. Andrew said, "I know, you have never heard of John 3:16 before." Stephen didn't say anything; he just held his hands up, gesturing guilty as charged. Then, the two men entered the vault.

Then in the darkness of the mine, Becky said to Andrew, "You had better get this one right!" Suddenly being shocked at herself that she had spoken that thought out loud. She put her hand over her mouth, indicating she had not intended to say that. She was silent afterward as the scene continued.

Andrew reached up and pulled the light switch chain illuminating the three items stored in the vault. He thought that he might as well start with who Jesus is to lay the groundwork for the rest of the items they were to inventory. Andrew said, "You see, Stephen, Jesus being God became a man by being born of a woman, and lead a sin-free life as an example for all of us to follow. He died becoming a sacrifice on this very cross that you see here." Then Andrew picked up the inventory clipboard and checked the box indicating that the Cross of Jesus was still available for all mankind who desire the blessings provided by the sacrifice Jesus made. Andrew said: "Here is the Veil that was torn when Jesus died while hanging on that cross. The veil tore in two pieces when Jesus died, signifying there would always be access to the holy of holies, that is the Holy Spirit." Then he checked the box, acknowledging that the Veil that was torn was still in the vault, allowing access to the Holy Spirit. Walking over to the other side of the vault, Andrew picked up a book off a table, indicating to Stephen that this was the last item of the day. Andrew said: "This is the Testimony of the New Covenant. This book contains all the promises of God as a result of the sacrifice Jesus made on the cross. This allows us to enter through the Veil and receive the gift of the Holy Spirit. We inventory the vault daily to ensure that its contents are always available." Then he checked off the last box on the inventory sheet.

Stephen said, "Alright, but what are the items in the main warehouse?" Andrew replied: "Stephen, those are your sins. They are to be destroyed and forgiven at the moment you are born again. Upon believing in the Lord Jesus Christ, who endured the cross, you will pass through the veil into the holy of holies, receiving the promise of the Holy Spirit, which is eternal life, which we refer to as salvation. This is the testimony of the New Covenant, and in it, you will abide in Jesus." Stephen was shocked! The warehouse was huge, and most of the boxes were very large. Stephen asked, "When will this happen?" Andrew showed Stephen the clipboard with the very date, hour, minute, and second that his conversion would occur. It also listed the price that Stephen was going to have to pay. Stephen said to Andrew, "But boss, you said, 'it was a gift!'" Andrew said: "Son, the Holy Spirit is a gift. Jesus Christ died for the ungodly. His death took away the sin of the world when He paid the price on the cross, purchasing you and me while we were still sinners. In Him, we have redemption through His blood, the forgiveness of sins." (I John 2:24-27, Acts 2:38-39, Acts 16:17, Hebrews 12:2, Romans 5:12-21, Colossians 1:13-14). Andrew continued: "The price that you must pay, Stephen, is the consequence of your sins in this warehouse. Whether or not a person is saved, they are still held accountable for their actions, like when someone gets caught stealing. The consequences are they have to go to court and pay a fine and make restitution. If they never pay for their crime, the government cannot forgive their infraction." (Ezekiel 33:12-16, Leviticus 6:1-5, Luke 19:1-10, Numbers 5:5-8).

Andrew continued: "Just remember some people have warehouses filled with unrepented sins that are two, three, or even as some five stories tall. Stephen, one of your sins is an affair that you will have on your wife. She will hold you accountable for your actions. At this point in your life, you will turn your heart to seek after God's truth, thus inspiring you to be born again. Your sin of infidelity will be forgiven by God. But you will need to pray for your marriage, asking your wife to forgive you. And yes, Stephen, the gift of God, the Holy Spirit, is free, thus reconciling us to God through a repentant heart. There are times in life when we have to correct the wrong that we have done to others even though God has forgiven us." At that, Stephen walked over to a large box marked 'MARRIAGE INDISCRETION.' He opened it and looked inside.

Then the camera turned off, and the mine was again filled with darkness. A few moments went by in silence before anyone dared to turn their headlamps back on. (Romans 5:6-11, I John 3:5, Ephesians 1:3-14, Psalms 103:11-12, Luke 19:1-10).

Discussion Questions:

1) Of the items inventoried in the vault, can you find them in the Old Testament? Can you locate their fulfillment in the New Testament? Answers below:
   a) The Cross of Jesus: Psalms 22, Numbers 21:4-9, II Kings 18:4, John 3:14-15.
   b) The Veil that was Torn: Exodus 26:31-35, Matthew 27:50-51.
   c) The Testimony of the New Covenant: Genesis 12:1-3, Genesis 22:1-8, Galatians 3:15-18.
   d) Jesus: Deuteronomy 18:15-18, John 1:45, Acts 3:22-23, John 20:24-29.

2) Stephen asked Andrew: "Who is this Jesus fella that you are talking about?" Can you give a detailed description of what Jesus represents to you?

3) The Holy Spirit is a free gift from God; the forgiveness of our sins is also available from God. Are there incidents,

indiscretions, or crimes in your past that you would still be held accountable by a friend, a loved one, or a governing body?

4) If you were to receive forgiveness from God, would any of the above [question 3] still hold you accountable?

5) If your sins, crimes, or indiscretions were never repented of, would these items prevent you from being saved?

Scriptures: John 3:16, I John 2:24-27, Acts 2:38-39, Acts 16:17, Hebrews 12:2, Romans 5:12-21, Colossians 1:13-14, Ezekiel 33:12-16, Leviticus 6:1-5, Luke 19:1-10, Numbers 5:5-8. Romans 5:6-11, I John 3:5, Ephesians 1:3-14, Psalms 103:11-12, Luke 19:1-10.

Discussion Question Scriptures: Psalms 22, Numbers 21:4-9, II Kings 18:4, John 3:14-15, Exodus 26:31-35, Matthew 27:50-51, Genesis 12:1-3, Galatians 3:15-18, Genesis 22:1-8, Deuteronomy 18:15-18, John 1:45, Acts 3:22-23, John 20:24-29.

Chapter 14

In the Gall of Bitterness

A cts 8:23 For I perceive that thou art in the gall of bitterness, and in the bond of iniquity. [KJV]
James 3:6 And the tongue is a fire, a world of iniquity. The tongue is so set among our members that it defiles the whole body, and sets on fire the course of nature; and it is set on fire by hell.

Nineteen Years Before the Events at the Cabin in the Way

"I do," said Jill Loper, and then Clark Williams slid a wedding ring onto her finger and leaned in to kiss his beautiful new bride. Soon, they purchased a new house and began to look for a church to call home. After visiting what seemed like hundreds of local churches, both small and large, the Williams's settled down at a quaint mid-sized church known as Truth Valley. After a few years, they became more active in the church, gaining the church staff's confidence, and became Sunday school teachers. Jill taught the fourth-grade girls and Clark, the second-grade boys. As the years went by, the Williams's continued to move up with the children. They were offered the position of youth pastors, of which they accepted.

Things were going well at church and work for Jill and Clark, but their home life was beginning to suffer. They were managing to keep their heads above water financially. After paying the mortgage on their four-bedroom house, there wasn't any money for their savings. Last year they added a minivan payment to their household budget.

Two Years Before the Events at the Cabin in the Way

Jill said to Clark, "We're going to be late for our appointment if you don't hurry up and get ready!" Clark was not happy that he had to take off from work again. He jumped into the shower, and he heard Jill yelling across the master bedroom, "ARE YOU KIDDING ME! WE DON'T HAVE TIME FOR YOU TO TAKE A SHOWER! WE ARE LATE! WE SHOULD HAVE LEFT ALREADY!"

Clark looked for his clean pair of pants as he walked around the bedroom, wearing only a towel. He said, "I told you last week today was going to be a bad day to go to the fertility center." Being calmer, Jill said, "I know, but today was the only day they could schedule us." Clark said, "I still don't understand why we can't look into adopting, even from a foreign country? It doesn't necessarily have to be a baby." He anticipated he wasn't going to get a response from his wife about adoption. Then Jill said, "I called the fertility center and rescheduled; we just lost 250 dollars on another missed appointment! Clark, do you know why we can't get pregnant?" When he didn't answer, Jill said, "That's why we are going to the center."

Two Weeks Later

It was a rare weekday morning when Jill and Clark had a day off together. They were having breakfast while watching an old black and white movie when the phone rang. "Hi," said the woman from the fertility center, "this is Karen, Dr. Gordon's receptionist. I have a 12:30 appointment that just opened up if you are interested." Jill turned the TV off and said to the woman, "We'll see you at 12:30, and this time, we'll even be early."

It was an hour drive to The Gordon Fertility Center. The Williams's had canceled two other appointments. Clark said, "Jill, I've been thinking a lot lately. It will be good for us to find out why you haven't been able to get pregnant." Jill looked at Clark and said, "I'm just going to remain optimistic."

After arriving at the center, Karen, Dr. Gordon's receptionist, said, "I have this packet for you to fill out, Mrs. Williams. Sir, this packet is for you." The two finished the paperwork and turned it back in. Then Jill and Clark were escorted into Dr. Gordon's office for a consultation. As the Williams's entered his office, they noticed he was an older gentleman who had experience in this area. Dr. Gordon came highly recommended through the Williams's health Insurance plan. "Good afternoon," said Dr. Gordon as he shook both Jill and Clark's hand. "I want to go over the procedures so we can determine what is preventing you two from getting pregnant."

Two hours later, the Williams's were back on the road and decided to stop at their favorite restaurant to grab some dinner, since it would be late when they got home. It had been raining most of the afternoon, and another band of showers was moving through. As Clark parked the car, he pointed out to Jill that he saw Sara Summers walking out of the Skeleton Crew Pub and Eatery with two men. Jill simply tucked that away in her heart. Then they made their way into the Dixie Day café.

Six Weeks After Testing at the Gordon Fertility Center

Jill and Clark once again found themselves sitting in Dr. Gordon's office. "Good afternoon, Mr. and Mrs. Williams," said Dr. Gordon. "I have the test results from last month." He handed an identical packet to both Jill and Clark, explaining in detail why it was that they haven't been able to get pregnant.

"Azoospermia," Jill said to her husband as they were lying in bed that same night. Then she said, "Well, it sure looks like I'm not the problem anymore." Holding the test results in her hand, she said, "Clark, turn the light off!" Then she said to Clark in the darkness, "Your count, as Dr. Gordon put it, is extremely low! So you see, my dear, that is why I haven't been able to get pregnant! Thank you so very much!"

A Few Weeks Later at Truth Valley Church

It was a beautiful Sunday morning at Truth Valley Church when Jill and Clark were in the Coffee Barn sitting at a corner nook table with another couple while Brenda and Daisy sat at a table behind them. Jill said to the other couple, "You know, I haven't seen Sara lately, it seems as though she has become quite the little backslider since her husband passed away. Bless her little heart, for trying so hard." The two couples talked back and forth, gossiping about various members of the congregation until it was time to go in the sanctuary to worship Jesus in spirit and in truth.

Clark continued to pursue his wife about adoption, but as the months went on, bitterness, strife, and envy began to grow between them. There was a peace that couldn't be found amid contention. Though searched for, it was not obtained. Though listened for, it was not heard. It was desired, but it remained unattainable. Love began to fade away and was only found in the un-swept corners. Joy had been abandoned and was no longer sought after. Kindness occurred only in the depths of sleep. Goodness and faithfulness were no longer companions. Gentleness had moved away. Tenderheartedness had turned her back on her friend, stomping out forgiveness like a fire that was no longer desired. Bitterness was sitting and reigning from her throne.

Six Weeks Before the Events at the Cabin in the Way

Jill and Clark had decided to step down as youth pastors at Truth Valley Church. Before making that announcement, Pastor James asked them to lead the youth group to the Cabin in the Deep Dark Woods. This was the annual camping and hiking trip and the highlight of all high school students at the church. Without any hesitation and forgetting about their resignation letter that was tucked away in his Bible, Clark accepted the new assignment to lead the annual youth camping expedition. Then without even looking at his wife, he could feel her cold stare. Later, before leaving the church parking lot, she asked him, "Have you lost your mind? CLARK, DO YOU NOT REMEMBER THAT WE DECIDED WE WERE GOING TO STEP DOWN THIS MORNING?!"

The Morning of the Camping Trip

"Is your bag ready, Jill?" Clark asked as he headed to the car with her following, locking the door behind them. As they drove to the church, there was an air of tension they could feel within their soul. Before arriving at the church, Jill broke the silence saying, "Look, those kids will pick-up on our anxiety. We have to get along for the next four days, even if we have to put on a show. This is their trip, and those kids are counting on us." A few moments went by, then Clark finely said, "Agreed." However, Clark still held a grudge for the resentment he felt Jill had towards him.

Discussion Questions:

1) At what point does a spoken word become gossip?
   Answer: Matthew 15:16-20. Also read from the Amplified version.
2) Where in the Bible is a comparison of gossip made?
   Answer: James 3:1-12.
3) Have you ever held a grudge against someone like Clark did in this chapter for something he perceived Jill was doing?

Scripture Section: Ephesians 4:31 Let all bitterness, wrath, anger, clamor, and evil speaking be put away from you, with all malice. [32]And be kind to one another, tenderhearted, forgiving one another, even as God in Christ forgave you.

Scriptures: Acts 8:23, James 3:6.

Discussion Question Scriptures: Matthew 15:16-20, James 3:1-12.

Chapter 15 ~ Sunday

The Two Builders and the Two Brothers

After the projector went off, the mine was dark again. It was Ranger Jim who broke the silence in the darkness with the click of his headlamp switch. Then all the campers turned their headlamps back on after the dramatic scene of Andrew and a stranger named Stephen unfolded before their eyes in the vault. Ranger Jim instructed the group to follow him back to the classroom. Everyone was quiet as they made their way out of the mine. They were engrossed by Becky and Andrew's portrayals that were displayed on the mine wall that morning. The walk back to the classroom was not only quiet, but it was uneventful. Clark extended his hand, indicating to Mark to handover the troublemaking device that Peter had brought with him on that day's excursion. However, when he did, Mark turned the filter dial to **"RM"** **(Repentance Mode)** without knowing it. Clark put the video camera in his backpack, tucking it securely on top.

As the youth group entered the classroom, they saw that the other rangers had prepared lunch. Everyone grabbed a sandwich, a small bag of chips, and a drink. Then they all sat down and began to eat. There was an air of silent tension that filled the room. It was as if everyone had been exposed to an overdose of truth; however, Brenda broke the silence.

The girls were sitting at a table, and Jill was within earshot. Brenda said to her two sisters and her best friend, "You know there's something to be said about a person who emulates the fruit of the spirit." She was indicating how her mother, Sara taught them more with her actions than with her words. Brenda continued, "Like Mom always said, 'Keep your eyes on Jesus, and everything will work out the way God has intended it to.'" She said that being the oldest and sensing that Jill was distancing herself from the girls. There was a noticeable hardening that had begun to show its true colors. It was as if Brenda had an awareness of what was tucked away in Jill's heart. Brenda remembered the day that she and her sister Daisy sat behind Jill and Clark's table at the church Coffee Barn. That was the day Jill said to the other couple, "You know I haven't seen Sara lately…" Speaking the name of Jesus over her two sisters and best friend, would, for the moment, shield them from the bitterness that was beginning to chip away the fabric of Jill's life and marriage.

Then Daisy said to the girls, "Not everyone has been portrayed in the video camera yet. The only ones we haven't seen are Peter and Mark. Has anyone else noticed that?" Lisa said, "I was just thinking the same thing." Both Becky and Brenda concurred with the two other girls. All four girls began to wonder why Peter and Mark hadn't had their time in the camera spotlight yet?

Then Ranger Jim stood in front of the classroom and announced he was going to show a movie that detailed the history of the school, the red covered bridge, and the mine and millworks company. It was a somewhat dated movie projector; the old reel to reel type with the 8 mm film. As the film began to roll and shine on the screen, the group was relieved that this movie projector was going to take precedence over Peter's video camera.

As the movie projector started, a man spoke in front of the office building and dormitory, before they had fallen down. He entered the building and began to share the history of the Edwardsville Mine and Millworks Company. Then, a loud clap of thunder was heard, just as a bolt of lightning struck the power pole outside the classroom window. This caused all power to be lost at the ranger station and the classroom. As the rain began to fall, a man wearing a hooded cloak made his way back into the deep dark woods. However, the movie continued, uninterrupted, despite the power outage due to the same hooded man's authority.

As the beam of light shone on the screen, it transitioned to a scene of fog rising off a creek bank on a cool summer morning as a stream of water trickled along the sand and the rocks. The wind began to blow, and the fog lifted away. Then the scene shifted to a baby nursery in a hospital. This scene had two baby beds with a baby in each one laying there with their blankets. The names Peter Myers and Mark Phillips were written on the baby beds, on golden plaques. Everyone was watching and began to laugh at the two babies who were cute as buttons. The scene began to blur and then went back in focus. The two boys were seen once again, sitting up in the baby beds. They distinctively looked like Pete and Mark, around the age of four. The two boys climbed out of their beds at the same time and walked into separate rooms where their families were gathered, having a birthday party for the two boys. The boys nor the families were aware of the other. Each boy got a birthday present from their mothers at the exact same time. Upon opening the gifts, they discovered that they were Bob the Builder outfits, and each one came with a helmet and tool belt. They put on their new matching outfits. The two boys had a great time and were loved by all in attendance at the birthday parties.

The scene faded to a blur as it shifted to a small creek bed with a trickle of water that ran along a sandy and rock-lined beach, where the sun was shining brightly, and a light breeze was blowing. The two boys, still four years old, were seen walking along the creek bank wearing their Bob the Builder outfits with the helmet and tool belt, but now they both had on little yellow work boots. They were walking along, not like a couple of children; instead, they had a serious and focused demeanor. They talked back and forth about something seemingly important. Soon, both boys had a set of blueprints in their possession, and shortly after that, they both stopped, finding a plot of land near the creek bank. They each staked out a land claim where they intended to build a house, each boy on their own parcel of land.

Peter and Mark began to build the foundations for their houses, each on their own property. Peter was building his foundation on the rock. In contrast, Mark chose a less expensive piece of land and built the foundation for his house on the sand. This would be quicker and cheaper to build. In time both houses were finished and looked great. Others came along later and bought into the neighborhood, building their own houses; some on the rock and others chose to build on the sand. The homes were all very similar in size. All was well in the Sandrock Creek Subdivision, for a while.

Peter and Mark both grew up and became men, with their own families. It would rain from time to time, but for the most part, the weather was mostly pleasant in Sandrock Creek. That was until the day the GREAT-GREAT storm hit and HIT HARD! The clouds in the north began to build with an intensity that had never been seen before. Peter and Mark knew that it was going to be extremely bad, but they could not have predicted the devastation that was to come. So, each man with his own family walked to their homes and took shelter. Peter thought that it was going to be bad, so he invited Mark and his family to stay at his house. Before he built his house, Peter was warned in a dream to build it on the rock. Mark had the same dream, but he disregarded it as foolishness. Mark heard Peter's invitation but did not respond. He lied in his own heart, saying to himself, "I can't hear you, Peter, because of the wind."

An old man named Noah yelled, "Repent of all your wickedness and lying to your own heart, for destruction is sure to come!" The rain began to fall, and soon the creek began to rise. The people of Sandrock Creek heard that old man over the wind and the rain; some families even left their sand foundation homes to take shelter in a house that was built upon the rock. Mark was one of those men that hardened his heart. Mark entered his house, built on the sand. His wife asked him, "MARK, should we take shelter with Peter in his house built on the rock?" Not answering her, Mark shut the door and locked it. As the storm raged through the night, the waters swept away every house in Sandrock Creek, built on the sand. Of all the residents who stayed in their homes built on the sand, only Mark survived, but his wife and children also perished in that great flood.

Matthew 7:24 "Therefore whoever hears these sayings of Mine, and does them, I will liken him to a wise man who built his house on the rock: 25 " and the rain descended, the floods came, and the winds blew and beat on that house; and it did not fall, for it was founded on the rock. 26 "But everyone who hears these sayings of Mine, and does not do them, will be like a foolish man who built his house on the sand: 27 " and the rain descended, the floods came, and the winds blew and beat on that house, and it fell. And great was its fall."

"That's rough," said Daisy. "I know," replied Lisa. All the girls discussed Mark's situation, and they had a deep feeling of despair over the loss of his family. Although only a movie, there was a hint of reality. Becky said in a whisper, "I could see that happening for real. Not the storm and flood, but that Peter would take care of his family. On the other hand, Mark could lose his wife and children to divorce or something." Mark and Peter were especially intrigued. Then Mark said to Peter as a tear was coming from his eye, "I didn't see that one coming." Indicating he was shocked over the loss of his entire family by building his home on the sand instead of the solid foundation of the Rock. And at that moment, Mark felt responsible for their deaths.

After the flood at Sandrock Creek, Peter set out to find his best friend Mark. After finding him, Peter moved his family to the Great Flat Plains of Wilderness Grass, two counties away. Peter and his wife had decided that it was too dangerous to live along the creek bank any longer. While living in Wilderness Grass, Peter purchased a plantation with a lot of land and became a shepherd. Mark bought a plantation across the street from Peter, and both men were prosperous in everything they did. Peter was a keeper of the sheep and Mark, a tiller of the ground (Genesis 4:1-15).

As the years went by in Wilderness Grass, Mark's bitterness increased toward Peter's prosperity. Mark blamed Peter for the loss of his entire family, even though he was the one who lied to his own heart about the Great-Great storm, knowing that he had built his house on the sand. Eventually, Mark's lie became truth to his heart.

At harvest time, Mark gathered his grain and corn and laid them out before God. Peter brought the best of his flock and offered them to God. God accepted Peter's offering. However, He did not recognize Mark's, which made him very angry. "Mark, be aware, sin will seek to destroy you," God said. Later that same day, while Mark and Peter were alone in a field, Mark looked at Peter and raised his hand with a weapon in it. Then with his hand raised in anger against his best friend Peter, Mark killed him. The projector continued to run, and God said, "Mark, the voice of Peter's blood cries out to Me from the ground. Why have you betrayed innocent blood?" (Psalms 10:8-11).

Discussion Questions:

1) What are the characteristics of your spiritual life? Are they the works of the flesh (on the sand), or the fruit of the spirit (on the rock)?

2) Reading the scripture Matthew 16:18-19, where Jesus speaks of the "rock," where else in the Bible can you find this "rock" mentioned?
   Answer: Ephesians 2:19-22 Jesus as the chief cornerstone, built on the Apostles and Prophets foundation. Revelation 21:14 and the wall of the city had twelve foundations with the twelve apostles of the Lamb written on them.

3) What have you given of yourself to the Lord as an offering? Is it self, or is it self-denial? Are you following after the voice of God like Peter or like Mark from this chapter?

4) Can you find in the Bible where the Apostle Paul states that there are two types of people, specifically the carnally minded and the spiritually minded?
   Answer: I Corinthians 7:17-24 and Colossians 2:11-15. There are more if you choose to dig deeper and search this out to its fullest.

Scriptures: Genesis 4:1-15, Psalms 10:8-11, Matthew 7:24-27.
Discussion Question Scriptures: Matthew 16:18-19, Ephesians 2:19-22, Revelation 21:14, I Corinthians 7:17-24 & Colossians 2:11-15.

Chapter 16 ~ Sunday

The Blood of the Lamb

Despite the power outage from the lightning strike earlier, the movie continued to play in the ranger station classroom, and all the campers were still attentively watching the film.

The scene abruptly shifted to a dinner party, there Jesus stood and gave a speech, "My friends, this bread that I break is My body," and He blessed the bread. Then He broke the bread and gave it to anyone who would receive it, saying, "Now eat." Looking up to heaven, Jesus held up the cup and said, "Father, this cup is My blood of the new covenant, which is shed for many for the remission of their sins." Then He took the cup and gave it to His disciples, saying," Drink from it, all of you. But I will not drink of this fruit of the vine from now until that day when I drink it new with you in My Father's kingdom." After that, they sang a hymn. Then, Jesus and His disciples went out to the Mount of Olives (Matthew 26:26-30).

As the host and guests left the dinner party, several people stayed behind who had volunteered to clean up. One of them was left sitting alone at the table. The other workers were tending to their responsibilities in various parts of the house. As the last guest left, Brad Summers stood up from the table and said: "My dear friends, worthy is the Lamb (Revelation 5:12). It was the Lamb of God, Jesus Christ, who chose before the foundation of the world to present His life as a living sacrifice for all mankind (Ephesians 1:3-4). It is by the precious blood of Jesus that we can be redeemed from a life of sin and death to a life of holiness. (I Peter 1:17-21, Romans 6:22). The fall of man in the third chapter of Genesis was a big deal, but it was not a surprise to God. The plan of salvation was established before the first man Adam was placed in the garden of Eden. The blood of bulls and goats was not sufficient to cleanse mankind from sin" (Hebrews 10:4). Brad said this while clearing the plates and cups from the table, taking them to Lisa and Daisy to clean in the back of the house. Brad paused for a moment and said, "Our Lord and Savior Jesus is being betrayed into the hands of sinful men as I speak" (Luke 24:7). He continued: "It was Jesus, who, being in the form of God, came into the world in the likeness of men. Having never sinned, He can redeem you and me from our sins. (Revelation 5:1-8, Philippians 2:5-11). Let us purify our souls in obeying the truth through the Spirit, and be born again through the word of God which lives and abides forever (I Peter 1:22-25). Open your eyes, turn from darkness to light, and from the power of Satan to God, that you may receive forgiveness of your sins and an inheritance among those who are sanctified by faith in Jesus Christ" (Acts 26:18). And with that last statement, Brad took the cup of the New Testament and drank from it. He placed it back on the table, and as he walked away, the cup fell over, spilling the remainder of the wine on the wooden table. Which signified that the blood of Jesus was being shed on the cross for the remission of sins. Then, the movie projector focused on the cup. The wine flowed from the table onto the floor, giving the youth group from the Truth Valley Church a visual of the blood of Jesus covering their own sins.

Andrew stood and addressed the group as the projector continued to show the cup of the new covenant. The wine flowed to the ground, and Andrew said, "Guys, does anyone know the significance of all that?" Andrew pointed to the screen where the wine was flowing onto the floor. Brenda answered, "When Jesus died on the cross, His blood cleansed us of our sins. The significance of the blood of the New Testament represented in that cup is that Jesus canceled our debt of sin by dying on the cross. Andrew replied, "Not only that, but the blood of Jesus voided the penalty of our sins (Colossians 2:11-15). However, we must still confess our sins, and Jesus is faithful and just to forgive us" (I John 1:7-9). Brenda said, "You mean like when John baptized Jesus and said, 'Behold! The Lamb of God who takes away the sin of the world?'" (John 1:29). Andrew said, "Without the shedding of blood there is no remission of sin (Hebrews 9:22). What I mean is this, when Jesus died on the cross, it was through His blood that redemption occurred."

Becky demanded, "Well then, Andrew, what does faith have to do with salvation if our sins are covered by the blood of Jesus?" Andrew replied, "You see, Becky, salvation is provided to everyone by the blood of Jesus, but we believe that Jesus' blood covers our sins through our faith." Becky asked, "Okay, Andrew, but how am I to know that I am a sinner?" Andrew answered: "Becky, the book of Romans says that all people have sinned and fall short of God's glory (Romans 3:21-26). However, His blood cleanses us from our unrighteousness when we confess that we are a sinner. When we say that we don't need the blood of Jesus to cover our sin, we deceive ourselves, and there is no truth in us" (I John 1:8-10). Becky again questioned Andrew, "But how, I mean, what do I have to do to be saved by the blood?" Andrew replied: "Salvation is a gift of God. We don't do anything to earn it (Ephesians 2:8-9). It is through His grace that Jesus provides salvation to you. We receive it by faith when we call upon the name of the Lord (Romans 10:9). You see, Jesus was rich and became poor, so everyone would have access to salvation through Him (II Corinthians 8:9). This is called mercy, and God grants us mercy because we have sinned in ignorance (I Timothy 1:12-17). Our hope and faith are in the Father's love and mercy, and it is by the resurrection of Jesus Christ from the dead that we can obtain salvation" (I Peter 1:3-5). Lastly, Andrew said, "Only the truth of God can make you free from a life of sin and deception" (John 8:31-32).

As Andrew finished speaking, the last of the wine spilled from the cup of the new covenant. Then there was a resounding cry heard from the back of the house where Lisa and Daisy were cleaning, and they lamented, "Oh God, they have crucified our Lord!"

The scene shifted three days ahead when Lisa and Daisy walked down a narrow path on the first day of the week. As the two women approached the tomb, there was an earthquake for an angel of the Lord descended from heaven and rolled away the stone and sat on it. The angel's robe was white as snow and looked like lightning. The angel said to Lisa and Daisy: "Don't be afraid, I know that you two came here seeking Jesus who was crucified. He is not here; for He has risen, just as He told you that He would. Come in and look and then go and tell His disciples that He has risen from the dead. You will see Him in Galilee when you go there." Then Lisa and Daisy went out quickly from the tomb with fear and great joy and ran to tell the disciples that Jesus had risen and was alive (Matthew 28:1-8).

About forty days later, Andrew and Brad watched as Jesus was taken up out of their sight, and a cloud received Him. Then a man said to them, "Why do you stand gazing up into heaven? This same Jesus, who was taken up from you into heaven, will so come in like manner as you saw Him go into heaven" (Acts 1:9-11).

Then from the movie screen, Peter said, "God has made Jesus, whom you crucified, both Lord and Christ." When Mark heard that, he was deeply troubled in his heart, he said to Peter, "What shall I do?" Then Peter answered Mark saying: "Repent, and be baptized in the name of Jesus Christ for the remission of sins; and you shall receive the gift of the Holy Spirit. For the promise of the Holy Spirit is to you and your children, and to all people who are called by our Lord and Savior Jesus Christ" (Acts 2:36-39).

Once again, the group was left speechless as the old movie projector ran out of film and began to go flap—flap—flap shining its light on the screen. The dust in the air was seen floating through the beam of light until Ranger Jim came back in the classroom and turned it off. Then the power to the building came back on, but the rain continued to fall in a steady downpour.

Discussion Questions:

1) Do you have confidence that the blood of Jesus has covered your sins?

2) Where does the Bible differentiate between walking in darkness and light?
   Answer: Acts 26:18

3) How does the blood of Jesus cleanse us from all sin?
   Answer: I John 1:5-7.

4) Do you know where in scripture, the Bible declares the power and authority that raised Jesus from the dead?
   Answer: Romans 8:11.

Scriptures: Matthew 26:26-30, Revelation 5:12, Ephesians 1:3-4, I Peter 1:17-21, Romans 6:22, Hebrews 10:4, Luke 24:7, Revelation 5:1-8, Philippians 2:5-11, I Peter 1:22-25, Acts 26:18, Colossians 2:11-15, I John 1:7-9, John 1:29, Hebrews 9:22, Romans 3:21-26, I John 1:8-10, Ephesians 2:8-9, Romans 10:9, II Corinthians 8:9, I Timothy 1:12-17, I Peter 1:3-5, John 8:31-32, Matthew 28:1-8, Acts 1:9-11, Acts 2:36-39.

Discussion Question Scriptures: Acts 26:18, I John 1:5-7, Romans 8:11.

Chapter 17 ~ Sunday

That Little Spinney Thing

After Ranger Jim turned off the movie projector, he explained his favorite part of the show. He said, "It was the part with the office building and dormitory just before the blizzard of '52. It was that storm which caused the building to collapse." He clarified that the cabin was used as an emergency shelter during the blizzard that same year. Which was why it had running water, a kitchen, and a bathroom. He added: "The townspeople didn't like going to the outhouse while a storm was raging outside. Years later, the parks department provided electricity to the cabin. Which began the era of renting it out to various groups and organizations." He said all that, knowing they didn't see the movie showing the history of the mine or cabin. Then he asked everyone to follow him for their next tour.

While walking, Ranger Jim guided the group through the millworks facility. As they walked, Clark began to worry that the video camera would come back on at any moment. It was in his backpack since he had taken it from Mark earlier. Clark couldn't begin to imagine what was going to transpire when Daisy used the video camera while in the **"RM" (repentance mode).**

Clark's mind had withdrawn into his own little world, and he began to think of everything that had happened in his own life. There was the billboard, he saw every day just before he turned into his subdivision. It said, "Quick Divorce For Men—call today for your free consultation: 1-5-5-5-D-I-V-O-R-C-E and get what your heart desires!" He was thinking about how everyone he knew would justify his reasons for divorcing Jill and receive their sympathy. He had even convinced himself that Jill's parents would say to him, "Clark, you will be better off without her and…"

"Clark—Clark—Mr. Williams, can you hear me?!" asked the ranger. Clark finally re-entered the real world. Then Ranger Jim said to him, "This is the end of our millworks tour," and then he shook Clark's hand. As Ranger Jim said his final goodbyes to the youth group from the Truth Valley Church, he had one more piece of advice for them. He said, "Hey gang, don't work too hard, but always remember to give them a honest days work." Ranger Jim had always been an honest man and a hard worker. As Ranger Jim Arnett walked outside, he put his hood over his head and then disappeared into the deep dark woods.

After finishing their tour of the millworks facility, the group walked outside. Andrew announced to everyone, "Hey guys, look, the sun is out." It had been raining all that day, and there was more rain looming over the horizon. As Jill walked outside of the millworks facility, a ray of sunshine hit her face. She put her arms straight out even with the horizon and tilted her head back ever so slightly, so the sun highlighted her face and hair. She began to spin around in a moment of bliss, taking in a rare beam of sunshine after mostly rain and gloom. Clark saw his wife and remembered the wedding photograph on his desk at work, the one he saw every morning. That moment was very similar to the one the wedding photographer caught. He remembered the first time he saw that picture of Jill and he thought in his heart, "She is the most beautiful woman to ever walk the face of the earth." He always called it "that little spinney thing." After years of bitterness, could there be a hint of love remaining in his heart for his wife? Clark felt a twitch in his heart as he watched her do that little spinney thing a moment ago. All the scenes of the weekend began to play out in Clark's head. He began to think as they made their way back to the cabin:

> Could that prayer of Daniel Edwards, from so long ago, still affect people at the cabin? "…that You pour out Your Spirit on the hearts of all." He was thinking of Lisa burning in hell when Jesus said to her, "I know you not." Could that fate be reserved for him or Jill? He thought how he blew it, trying to interpret Revelation 3:20 and then Andrew's speech of Jesus being outside the church. He felt that his rendition of the kingdom parables was a turning point until he saw Jill wearing a prison uniform in the flames of hell. When Sarah washed the feet of Jesus, he remembered he was responsible for the rumor about her walking out of that bar. He replayed that scene where Pastor James was standing before Jesus, and indignation was found in his heart. Clark began to acknowledge that he had a great deal of resentment in his own heart. He pleaded with the Lord to take it from him; it was becoming a burden that was more than he could bear. Clark's mind continued to debate: Is the Cross of Jesus, the Veil that was torn, and the Testimony of the New Covenant still available for him and Jill? Was his marriage built on the sand, or was it built on the Rock? Was he his wife's keeper, or would he betray her someday? And that video camera; what was that all about? How did it get put back together? "That sure is a lot to wrap my head around," Clark said to himself as he walked along.

As the group continued their hike, Clark fell slightly behind the others. Once again, his thoughts were running amuck at the events that happened over that weekend. Looking ahead as he saw a ray of sunshine shimmering off the back of Jill's hair, Clark thought, "Oh, what a beautiful woman she is." Instead, he said that out loud, not realizing that Lisa heard him say it, as the rest of the group was slightly ahead and talking about the tour of the millworks facility. A light rain began to fall, and the cabin was still ten minutes away. Clark was unaware that one of those men wearing a hooded cloak had been following him. A scripture came into his mind: Husbands, love your wives, even as Christ also loved the church, and gave himself for it (Ephesians 5:25).

Heidi Loper picked up the mail; she had forgotten to check the mailbox all weekend. She put the mail and packets on the dining room table. Heidi said hi to Flippers the cockatiel, and she asked him, "How are you today, baby? Do you need more food and water?" As the front door closed behind Heidi, a scene replayed in her head from last week while talking to her sister Jill Williams on the phone. Heidi remembered hearing Clark say in the background, "Hey Jill, don't forget to ask your sister Heidi to get our mail for us while we are at the cabin next weekend."

Discussion Questions:

1) Can you imagine what it would be like to watch one of your loved ones burning in the flames of hell, knowing they would endure this agony never having relief? What steps could you take to solidify the gospel message to them?

2) Can you think of a passage in the Bible where a man lifted his eyes being in torments?
   Answer: Luke 16:19-31—the rich man and Lazarus. After reading this passage: would you prefer to live a life of bliss and wealth, then spend an eternity in the lake of fire because you denied the Lord Jesus? Or would you rather live a life of poverty and persecution and spend eternity with Jesus in His kingdom?

Scriptures: Revelation 3:20, Ephesians 5:25.
Discussion Question Scriptures: Luke 16:19-31.

Chapter 18 ~ Sunday

The Table of Repentance

All the hikers made their way back to the cabin as the rain was steadily falling. Everyone placed their backpacks at the front of the cabin, where the hanger hooks and coat rack was except for Clark. His mind had been preoccupied since they began their tour of the millworks facility. Clark's backpack was rather old and dated; it was his father's before him. It had a double leather strap and buckle fastener. Clark never used it since one of the straps had broken and fallen off years ago. He put his backpack on a chair by the kitchen table, not giving it another thought. Clark was again preoccupied, this time with turning the cabin over to the parks department the next morning.

That last night was the girls turn to cook dinner since the boys had made all the meals so far. It was the last night of the trip, so the girls decided to make the rest of the chicken, and they put out all the leftovers. After a while, there was a small feast being prepared in the cabin. Soon after, Becky rang the cowbell, and it didn't take long for the boys to gather around the counter and fill up their plates. They all tore into their food, and before long, all that was left on the table were empty dishes and half a pitcher of iced tea and lemon-aide. Then they began to discuss the events that transpired over the weekend.

Becky shared with the group that she went to see a play some time ago called, *The Scoundrel and the Lion's Lair*. It was a story about an immoral hunter and several of his corrupt friends. They were on a quest to hunt down a virtuous lion with a bow and arrow. After a few days of tracking the lion, they were hot on his trail, having found his fresh tracks along the riverbank in the mud. They decided to make camp for the night and to rise early the next morning and move in for the kill. As the others finished their meal, the main character, Mr. Hopkins, went for a stroll, and found himself face to face with his prey. However, he had left his bow and arrow at camp, and his friends were too far away to be of assistance.

"What happens next?" Daisy asked, intrigued. "Well, that's where the curtain falls in the theater," Becky said. Then Brenda said, "Oh yes, I remember, I took you to see that play. The main character, Mr. Hopkins, was face to face with the lion at the intermission." Becky, knowing that she had everyone's attention asked, "Anyone for some pie?" "I'll take some," Mark said. "Oh no, you don't," said Lisa indicating that she wasn't going to let Becky off the hook that easy. Lisa continued, "You can't leave us hanging with Mr. Hopkins looking into the eye of the lion and just go and get some apple pie. You need to finish the story!" "Okay, okay," Becky said with a chuckle as she began to finish the story.

Becky continued, "The curtain opens after the intermission and there in center stage…" as Becky began to speak, she was overcome by emotions. She remembered the scene, but suddenly, she was overwhelmed, and for the first time, she realized its true meaning. A few moments went by, and everyone was torn between the story and the emotions that Becky was displaying. Brenda said to Becky, "You know, I can finish the story for you." "No. I'll do it," Becky said, as she regained her composure, then she said:

The curtain opened with the lion and Mr. Hopkins still face-to-face and looking into each other's eyes. Then the lion said to Mr. Hopkins, "I am a virtuous

Lion, and you, Sir, are a liar, a thief, and a robber. Why have you approached Me without showing Me any honor?" Knowing that he was full of corruption and deceit, Mr. Hopkins was filled with great fear, knowing that he could not overcome the Lion by his own merits or strength. He fell to his knees and said: "I have nothing to offer You. I am but a lowly scoundrel and You are a Lion highly favored among men, so please, please show me mercy! So, the Lion, being full of grace, reared up on His hind legs, and with a swipe of His massive paw, He put Mr. Hopkins on the ground and said, "I will show you mercy by granting you repentance." Then Mr. Hopkins began to weep before the Lion, displaying humility for the first time in his life. The Lion said: "I will take your vile nature from you as long as you follow after My standard of righteousness and do as I have always done in love of My fellow man. Now go and tell the others what has happened here and be My disciple, always seeking after the truth that is in Me" (Matthew 28:18-20).

Mr. Hopkins rejoined the others and told them everything that had transpired with the Lion. One of the men asked, "What should we do?" Mr. Hopkins said: "The Lion full of grace said to me, 'Repent and let every one of you be baptized in the name of Jesus Christ for the remission of sins; and you shall receive the gift of the Holy Spirit'" (Acts 2:38).

Becky and Brenda filled everyone in on the remainder of the play emphasizing how the men discussed the encounter with the Lion throughout the night. Then a discussion occurred at the table of repentance. The group discussed back and forth the value of presenting themselves humbly before God in love. Andrew referred to the Apostle Paul's statement in I Corinthians 13:13. He said, "We are to think more highly of love than the other characteristics of this verse. Although faith and hope are great qualities, love is the greatest."

Then Daisy got up to check on the coffee brewing in the kitchen and poured herself a cup. While walking back to the table, she bumped into the chair that Clark's backpack was sitting on, knocking it to the floor and spilling the items on top. While kneeling down on one knee to pick up the items, Daisy realized that she had the video camera in her hand. Opening the camera video screen, she began to film those sitting at the table, and this is what she saw as Mark had left it in the **"RM" (repentance mode).**

As she watched the video screen alone, Daisy saw the Lion of the tribe of Juda standing next to Jill, along with Satan. Satan was accusing her, pointing out the vileness of her nature. Then the Lion of the tribe of Juda rebuked the devil and Satan; as a result, he spoke no more. Jill was clothed in the wickedness of her nature alone before the Lion of the tribe of Juda. She felt corruption churning and stirring, emanating from her center in a virtually unexplainable mannerism. Then the Lion of the tribe of Juda spoke to those that were witnesses and said: "Behold, I take the vileness and filth of Jill's nature that ravaged her, and I will remove it. I will create a new and beautiful white garment to cover her with My nature. Jill, your sin of bitterness, gossip, and unforgiveness, will pass away." Then the Lion of the tribe of Juda, looking at Jill, warned her: "You must follow My ways and keep My command, then you will be given responsibilities over those things that belong to Me. I will let you, if you continue in My ways, to have your place with those that stand with Me" (Zechariah 3:1-7).

Then another scene began to unfold to Daisy's amazement as the Lion of the tribe of Juda continued speaking, He said: "I know those who are Mine. Let Jill, who calls on My name for salvation depart from iniquity. She shall pursue righteousness, faith, love, and peace with those who call on Me out of a pure heart. And a servant of Mine must not quarrel but be gentle to all, able to teach, patient, in humility correcting those who are in opposition. I will grant Jill repentance so that she may know the truth and that she may come to her senses and escape the trap of the devil, having been taken captive by him to do his will (II Timothy 2:19-26). The sacrifices that I accept are a broken spirit, a broken and a contrite heart, these I will not reject" (Psalms 51:17 NLT). And at that, the video camera suddenly shut off as if the battery had died.

Daisy, being a little surprised by what she saw, stuffed the few items still on the floor back into Clark's backpack. Then, picking up her coffee cup along with Clark's backpack and the video camera, standing up, she placed it back on the chair. Then she put the video camera back on top folding the flap over like it was, and she sat back down at the table. Daisy began to sip her coffee, not saying a word to anyone, since no one saw what had happened with the backpack or the video camera.

Lisa, who had also gotten up from the table while Daisy was watching the video camera, returned. Then Lisa, standing behind Jill, put her hands on Jill's shoulders and said, "Mrs. Williams, you know we all love you." And with that, Jill broke as she began to weep bitterly. Deep down, she was a very good woman who had been under a heavy strain in her life for many years, building a wall of bitterness towards people that didn't deserve it. All of the campers gathered around Jill as she continued to pour her heart out before God.

As this was happening, Daisy made her way back over to Clark's backpack and pulled the video camera out once more. She opened the view screen, pointing it at Jill as she was weeping in godly sorrow and having the baptism of repentance flowing over her. *And looking at the video screen for only a moment, Daisy abruptly slammed it closed just as her brother Brad was locking eyes with her.* And then she shoved it deep down into Clark's backpack folding the flap back over the contents. Then Daisy joined in with the others who were praying over Jill. Daisy was clearly shaken by what she saw the second time she held the video camera. She began to pray and weep over Jill, but Brad sensed that something else had caused her deep distress. Daisy looked over at Brad, knowing that he was the only one who saw her looking through the video camera that second time.

Discussion Questions:
1) Are you following the commands of God and keeping His standards? Do you have any idea what these maybe?

Answer: Acts 15:18-20, Mark 12:28-34, and II Corinthians 3:1-3.

2) Is there any place in the Bible that speaks on the new covenant standard of God?

Answer: Acts chapter 15, Mark 12:28-34, and II Corinthians 3:1-35.

3) Can you think of an example of a man in the Bible that was warned that the devil wanted to sift him like wheat?

Answer: the denial Luke 22:31-34, and Peter's restoration John 21:15-19. (Note: most Bible translations use the term sift in this passage). Try reading Luke 22:31 in multiple translations of the Bible.

4) If you continue in My ways. This statement was taken from Zachariah 3:7. Are you continuing to walk in the ways of the Lord Jesus?

Scriptures: Matthew 28:18-20, Acts 2:38, I Corinthians 13:13, Zechariah 3:1-7, II Timothy 2:19-26, Psalms 51:17.

Discussion Question Scriptures: Acts chapter 15, Mark 12:28-34, II Corinthians 3:1-35, Luke 22:31-34, John 21:15-19, Zachariah 3:7.

Chapter 19 ~ Monday

You Awake Bro

It was deep in the night, that time between too late and too early; when the crickets had already gone to sleep and the birds were not awake yet. There was a stillness in the deep dark woods. Outside the cabin, a couple of men wearing hooded cloaks were moving about as if they were on a mission.

In the cabin, in the darkness, while lying on his bed looking at the ceiling, Mark asked Peter in a whisper, "Peter, you awake, bro?" A few moments went by, and when Mark didn't receive the anticipated response from his best friend, he moved closer. Sitting on Peter's bed, he asked again, "Peter, you awake, bro?" Peter was usually dreaming at this time of the morning. He began to hear a voice in his dream and was floating over his body. Looking down, he saw that his mother was sitting on the side of his bed. He could hear her saying, "Dude, I need you to wake up bro, I have to talk to you." And at that, Peter's mother began to shake his shoulders in his dream, saying, "Wake up, man, can you just wake up and talk to me for a minute?" Peter came to his senses, with only one eye opened and barely able to see out of the other one, but knowing who it was that was sitting on his bed. He spoke to his best friend rather gruffly, since compassion was not going to awake for a few more moments. Peter said, "WHAT DO YOU

WANT?!" In that whisper, that is really shouting as the dream of his mother vanished into the night. "Peter, I have a problem, and I need to talk to you about it," Mark said that with his head down as if he were shrouded in shame. Peter half-awake, knowing in his heart, what was unfolding at that moment was going to be one of those life talks that could make or break a friendship. So, Peter, sensing that this conversation was going to be deep and personal, said to Mark, "Alright, alright, just let me wake up a little more so I can focus."

As Peter got out of bed, he grabbed his hoodie that was on the floor. Then taking Mark's arm, he began to lead him to the front door, thinking it would be better served to have this conversation outside in a private setting. Mark, knowing that Peter was taking him outdoors, said, "Are you crazy man, it's freezing cold out there," in a subtle shouting whisper. Peter looked around the cabin and saw that everyone was still sleeping. He realized that he had just moments to find a private place in this old one-room schoolhouse for Mark to open up to him. Then it came to him in the darkness as he was beginning to wake up and come to his senses. So, he whispered to Mark, "We are going to have to talk in the bathroom." The bathroom was the only place in the cabin where anyone could find privacy. As Peter and Mark entered the bathroom, they unintentionally left the door slightly open. This caused the light to shine in Brenda's eyes while lying on her bed.

Peter was fully awake and ready to listen to his friend. He said to Mark, "So, what's on your mind?" A long pause filled the air, and tears begin to pour down Mark's cheeks. Peter understood that this was going to be deeper than he could have imagined. He just waited for Mark to speak when he was ready. It was a time set aside for the heart to become tender so that the thoughts and intents of the heart could come out. After a while, Mark began to speak, saying to Peter, "Ever since my parents died, I have had a problem with pornography. It was just on occasion, then it developed into a deeper habit, and now it's all that I think about. I know it's wrong, but I just can't stop it on my own."

Peter listened intently as Mark continued to open up to him in detail about his addiction. He began searching for the most appropriate response. He was firmly entrenched in this life moment with his best friend, knowing the next words that came out of his mouth would be make it or break it words. Peter began to draw on his knowledge, having no experience in counseling anyone, much less someone with an addiction to pornography. Then he remembered a sermon Associate Pastor Arron Carpenter preached on purity, love, and holiness in the context of marriage.

"Mark, we all have a deep desire towards the opposite sex that was instilled in us during the creation (Genesis 1:28). This was given as a command from God to replenish the earth," said Peter. Then he continued: "Your pornography addiction is a perversion of that command from God that attracts men and women to each other. So, the things you view and feel are only partly based on truth, becoming nothing more than a lie. You see, it is the perversion of the devil and Satan, our accuser, who has masterminded this attack on your mind and soul, causing you to turn away from the purity and holiness of a woman which can only be found in loving a woman within the sanctity of marriage. This is what God originally intended when he created the first man and woman, placing them in the garden of Eden. It was this first man and woman whose marriage was ordained by God before the curse (Genesis 2:21-25). Their marriage was still in effect when they entered their new land outside the garden of Eden (Genesis 4:1). So, you see, Mark, it will only be through prayer, reading the Bible, and establishing your life on truth, that a life of purity, love, and holiness will develop. It is the word of God, through the Holy Spirit, washing over your flesh nature that will cause this perversion of the intended purpose of a woman to pass from your mind" (Matthew 19:4-6). As Mark listened intently to his friend's advice and wisdom, he said, "You're right, but I'm going to need your help. Will you be my accountability partner to help keep me from falling back into this perversion?"

And then after a little more advice from Peter, Mark said, "Thanks for listening, I really needed to tell you that and hear what you had to say." Since Peter thought they were through, he was about to get up off the bathroom floor and go back to bed, but he decided to ask Mark one more question. Peter asked, "Is there anything else on your mind?" Once again, the tears begin to stream down Mark's face. But this time, he began to sob inconsolably and laid his head on Peter's shoulder. Then Mark wrapped his arms around his best friend's neck and continued to sob. Once again, Peter was locked in another moment where he must be silent while Mark was weeping as his heart became tender once more, but this time it was deeper, much deeper.

Unknown to both Peter and Mark, Brenda was awakened by the light from the bathroom that was shining in her eyes after the boys left the bathroom door partially opened. Brenda was the last one to enter the cabin on Friday evening and claim a bed; she was stuck with the one by the bathroom door. As Brenda lay awake in her bed, she could hear everything Peter and Mark had discussed. Laying there silently, she was unable to do anything but listen and hope that Peter would find all the right words.

After a long while of weeping and sobbing, Mark finally gained some composure and blurted out, "I just want to kill myself!" Then Mark burst back into a deep sob, and that statement also broke Peter. He too began to weep and sob, being overwhelmed by this latest confession from his best friend.

Brenda realized that Peter's love for his friend was going to be a hindrance for him to council Mark on this new issue. So, she got out of bed, went into the bathroom, and then kneeling down on both knees, she took Mark's hands in hers, trying to gain his attention. Not worried that the others were still sleeping, she said to him, "Listen to me, Mark, listen to me…"

Discussion Questions:

1) Have you ever had a situation in your life where a friend approached you and had something important to talk about? In these types of situations, there is not always time to prepare your thoughts and develop an action plan. If this has ever happened to you, how did you handle the situation?

2) Can you think of any consequences of being addicted to pornography that could have adverse effects on your family, your friends, or your job?

3) Starting with photographs, then moving on to videos: what do you think pornography could lead to? And where is the endpoint of pornography, if there is one?
4) Can you find in the Bible where pornography is a sin?
Answer: Matthew 15:17-19, I Thessalonians 4:1-8, Romans 1:28-32.
5) What is the remedy for pornography from the Bible?
Answer: Ephesians 1:3-14, I John 1:7-9, II Peter 1:5-11.

Scripture Section: Pornography in the Bible: Numbers 25:1-9, I Corinthians 10:1-13, I Corinthians 6:18-20, Romans 6:5-14.

Scriptures: Genesis 1:28, Genesis 2:21-25, Genesis 4:1, Matthew 19:4-6.

Discussion Question Scriptures: Matthew 15:17-19, I Thessalonians 4:1-8, Romans 1:28-32, Ephesians 1:3-14, I John 1:7-9, II Peter 1:5-11, Numbers 25:1-16, I Corinthians 10:1-13, I Corinthians 6:18-20, Romans 6:5-14.

Chapter 20 ~ Monday

Listen To Me

Brenda was a strong young woman and a senior in high school. She had known Peter and Mark since they were in grade school. In fact, all of the kids on this trip had known each other since grade school, except Andrew. He moved to town when he was in middle school. Brenda knew Mark before his parents died. Mark's mother Martha died while he was in the sixth grade, and his father Glenn died during the summer before he started his freshman year of high school. Mark had to live with his grandmother after his dad died. She did everything possible to provide for him, but her age caught up with her, and her health issues had also taken a toll.

It was Brenda who encouraged Andrew to turn his life over to God when he was a sophomore. Brenda also encouraged Becky to attend church with her. Mark and Peter were both a year behind Brenda, being juniors. Brad and Daisy were both juniors, and they were also fraternal twins. Lisa was a freshman who had gotten special permission to attend that trip with her siblings. It was reserved almost exclusively for the juniors and seniors. Brenda always said about Peter and Mark, "Those two are like brothers; you just can't separate them." Peter and Mark were both an only child, giving them a special bond of friendship that made most people who knew them to think they acted like brothers. Mark drifted off thinking about the first meeting with Brenda in elementary school, as he was still sitting on the bathroom floor with his hands in hers, at the Cabin in the Way.

Seven Years Ago While in Elementary School

It was a hot Friday afternoon at William Tyndale Elementary School. All the students were outside on the playground while the school was having their annual field day event. Peter and Mark were in the fourth grade and had just started school there several months back. Peter began after winter break ended and Mark just a little before spring break that same year. Since those two boys were the new kids in school, they started a friendship that became their bond. They were like two peas in a pod.

"You just can't separate those two," said Brenda, a fifth-grader that year, who was running one of the game booths on the playground. Brenda asked, "Hey! Do you two boys want to play ring toss and win a prize?" Then she asked them, "Are you two in my sister Daisy's science class?" "Yes, we are," said Peter and Mark at the same time. Mark added, "I would like to play ring toss." "Okay then, take these rings and toss them onto any of those bottles over there. Oh, and don't cross this line," said Brenda as she grabbed both of Mark's hands, saying, "Mark, you have got to listen to me and pull yourself together." This woke everyone up at the Cabin in the Way, but she had finally gotten his attention. Then she said, "Listen to me, I've got you. Mark, I've got you."

Mark again focused on where he was, still not looking at Brenda, but rather staring at the bathroom floor as the memories of the school playground faded away. Daisy and Andrew came into the bathroom, got Peter up, and escorted him to the kitchen table, where the others were gathered. Peter was still visibly upset. Clark and Jill entered the bathroom and knew Brenda was best suited to handle this situation. She was helping Mark to calm down and made progress at gaining his attention and trust. Mark said, "I'm so embarrassed, I'm just so embarrassed. I can't believe this is happening to me." Clark not knowing what triggered this event but aware that the issue was suicidal thoughts. Clark said, "It's okay Mark, its good when things like this come out, so it can be dealt with." Now Brenda had a plan of action that was developing in her head. It was her longtime friend who had thoughts of ending his life.

As Mark regained his composure, Brenda said to him. "I remember seeing something called the Suicide Journal Instruction to the Way of Life." Brenda continued, "It had a goal of extending someone's life by five days. They suggested having someone journal their feelings and then read their responses every day for five days. It had three steps. Mark, are you with me?" Mark, almost completely composed, said, "Yes," with a slight sob.

"Mark, first, you must admit that you have thought about suicide, which I just heard you tell Peter. Is that true?" Brenda asked. Mark nodded his head in agreement, again trying to keep his composure. "Alright, now I want you to look me in the eyes," Brenda said. She asked Jill to get her a tablet and a pencil. Jill soon returned and handed them to her. Jill and Clark joined the others at the kitchen table, leaving Brenda to talk with Mark privately. After taking the tablet, she turned her attention back to Mark. "Do I have your eyes? I want your eyes to look at me and focus on my eyes. I've got you, but you have to trust me," Brenda said as she pleaded with him. "I'm going to give you this tablet, it's just an ordinary writing tablet, and you're going to write down your thoughts, alright, Mark?" She handed him the tablet and pencil, and he took them. Brenda was still looking into Mark's eyes as she said to him, "Now I want you to write down your thoughts by answering three questions." Then Brenda asked Mark these three questions:

Question 1: Can you wait until tomorrow to take your life? Now write your answer in your journal stating why you can live another day.

Question 2: You will do this one starting tomorrow. You will read your entry from today and ask yourself: Is my situation any less desperate? You will journal on day two, three, four, and five just as you did on day one, but you will also read all of your journal notes every day.

Question 3: On the fifth day, after reading your journal notes from the past four days, you will ask yourself: Is there any improvement in my will to live, and do I feel my life has value based upon my previous four days of journal notes?

After Brenda asked him those questions, Mark wrote down his thoughts in the journal for day one. Brenda's heart was revealed to Mark through her face and eyes. As the sun began to rise at the Cabin in the Way, Mark began to see the value in himself once more. Building a bathroom in the cabin provided the needed privacy and shelter for Mark in his hour of desperation. Where did that decision to build a bathroom come from anyway?

See Appendix D for the complete document: Suicide Journal Instruction to the Way of Life.

Discussion Questions:
1) Have you ever thought about ending your life due to depression or some other reason? Would you like to use the Suicide Journal that is found in appendix D?
2) Do you know anyone that presents suicidal thoughts or actions? Would you like to give them the Suicide Journal found in appendix D?
3) Can you think of any place in scripture where the Bible speaks about suicide?
    Answer: Exodus 20:13, Matthew 5:21, Genesis 1:26-27. See also Matthew 27:3-10, Acts 1:15-20, Psalms 55:23.

Scriptures: none.

Discussion Question Scriptures: See Discussion Question 3.

National Suicide Prevention lifeline: 1-800-273-8255

Chapter 21

The Outhouse

T he decision to build the bathroom that provided the needed privacy for Mark Phillips came during a town hall meeting a long time ago. BANG—BANG—BANG: went the gavel as the mayor of Edwardsville, Jacob Vandenberg, was trying to bring that meeting to order. It had not started, and chaos was beginning to run rampant in the council chambers.

It was Saturday morning, May 3, 1952. The town council of Edwardsville met the first Saturday of every month to discuss new business. Being such a small community, these gatherings were usually social in nature since not much ever happened in Edwardsville. However, that meeting was on the minds of all the residents. That was the day the blizzard of '52 was going to be discussed. And more specifically, the issue of the families having to take their children to the outhouse during that storm. They used a rope as a guide tied to an eye bolt screwed into the doorpost of the School in the Way that led them to the outhouse. That freak storm lasted two-and-a-half-days from April 9th through the 11th 1952. Jeffery Maxwell was the most vocal resident about the events that transpired at the School in the Way. He was the widower who had three children who were sick while the storm ravaged the town. He took his children to the outhouse every time that nature called in their illness. His wife Rachel had died in a freak accident soon after the birth of their third child, Jeffery Jr., when she was cleaning out their horse stable. She walked behind their horse Colonel, and he kicked her in the head, knocking her unconscious. She never regained consciousness and passed away about an hour and a half later. It was determined that she had died of a massive brain bleed. Jeffery was an excellent husband and a loving father. He made a solemn vow to himself and his late wife Rachel that this would not happen again to anyone in Edwardsville. So much had transpired during the storm that caused his children to be exposed to the weather elements. And he remained steadfast on his decision.

BANG—BANG—BANG: "ORDER, there will be order in this meeting," once again declared Mayer Vandenberg. Jeffery had been yelling profanities, directing them at the mayor and town council most of that morning. Then, as he was approaching the front of the assembly hall, it was as if he were going to take them all out. He was within a few feet of the mayor and council, still yelling profanities while heading towards them rather quickly when he was stopped. Jeffery was a rather large man with a stout build, and it took five men to restrain him and escort him outside before anything worse could happen. Jeffery was soon brought home by his brother-in-law and trusted friend Rodney Carmichael. Rodney gave his word to the town council, ensuring Jeffery would stay home for the remainder of the day so that the sheriff would not have to become involved.

"Skinny" Clyde Stallard, one of the councilmen, suggested to Mayor Vandenberg that they postpone the meeting until next month so everyone could settle down and be more attentive to the issue. The mayor was emphatic that the issue was going to be resolved before anyone left the meeting that day. Soon the meeting was brought to order, and the only item that needed to be discussed was the safety concerns that Jeffery Maxwell had with the outhouse at the School in the Way. After the meeting, the minutes were posted on the assembly hall's bulletin board, and this was the outcome.

On this day, Saturday, May 3, 1952, the Town Council of Edwardsville made an emergency declaration that the School in the Way shall have a kitchen, a bathroom, and running water provided. This will be part of a renovation so the facility could be used as a shelter for Edwardsville residents who may have need thereof.

That being an emergency declaration enacted by the mayor and town council, there were no funds available to complete the project. All materials and labor were to be donated. A sign-up sheet was included with the declaration page. After having made such a scene, Jeffery was the first one to sign up as a volunteer. Soon enough, all the building materials had been donated. When the day came to start working, only a handful of townspeople showed up. The project dragged on for several months; however, Jeffery was there every Saturday to give his time.

It was one of those work Saturdays when another band of rain was moving through. Jeffery and Rodney decided to work inside that day due to the weather and were taking a break. They were close to finishing the bathroom door's installation when, out of the blue, Rodney asked Jeffery, "Hey brother, do you know Jesus?" Jeffery had spent many hours on this project working with Rodney. When he asked the question about Jesus, they were sitting on the bathroom floor at the School in the Way. There was a peaceful curiosity that filled Jeffery's mind when asked the question about Jesus. Jeffery's wife had been a Christian, and she prayed for him every day before her death. So, that same bathroom that provided the privacy for Mark Phillips was also the place where Jeffery Maxwell turned his life over to Jesus many years earlier. It wasn't long after that day that Jeffery began to instill the belief of God into his children's lives so they would grow up as believers in Christ the Lord.

Therefore, the storm of '52, which caused such a hardship for so many people, became a blessing for so many more. The prayer of Daniel Edwards was still making its way boldly before the throne of grace. Thus providing the needed privacy for Mark Phillips that would be necessary so many years in the future.

Consequently, the late Pastor Edwards's prayer was still at work at the Cabin in the Way. It was his deep desire to build the Church in the Way that caused him to pray, "That all who enter this cabin should be blessed by the Holy Spirit so that they would follow after the ways of God." The townspeople of Edwardsville eventually completed the church that Daniel was unable to finish before his untimely death. They converted it into a one-room schoolhouse and named it the School in the Way, later becoming known as the Cabin in the Deep Dark Woods (John 17:1-26).

Discussion Questions:

1) This chapter emphasizes that peoples' prayers make their way to God by highlighting that He provides for them. For example, Jeffery built the bathroom, which Mark would need years later for privacy to confide in Peter and Brenda. Do you know of any situations similar to this one? (Revelation 5:8-10, Revelation 8:3-4).

2) Can you think of a place in the Bible that talks about having faith that God answers prayer?
   Answer: Ephesians 6:18, John 17:1-26, Matthew 7:7-8, Psalms 66:16-20, I John 5:14-15, Matthew 21:20-22, Psalms 6:8-10, Matthew 5:1-12, {Joel 1:1 & 2:28-32, Acts 2:17-21}.

3) Do you think that (prayers/teachings) may still be effectual, even after death? As was the case with Jeffrey's wife, Rachel, who had died before he surrendered his life to Jesus.
   Answer: John 17:1-26, Jude 20-22, John 14:12-18, John 16:5-15, Hebrews 9:1-28, Matthew 12:33-37, {Luke 23:32-34 & 39-46}, Psalms 22:1-31, Jonah 1:1-3:4.

Note: God provided for Nineveh through Jonah, like Jeffrey provided for Mark by building a bathroom.

Scriptures: none.

Discussion Question Scriptures: Revelation 5:8-10, Revelation 8:3-4, Ephesians 6:18, John 17:1-26, Matthew 7:7-8, Psalms 66:16-20, I John 5:14-15, Matthew 21:20-22, Psalms 6:8-10, Matthew 5:1-12, {Joel 1:1 & 2:28-32, Acts 2:17-21}, Jude 20-22, John 14:12-18, John 16:5-15, Hebrews 9:1-28, Matthew 12:33-37, {Luke 23:32-34 & 39-46}, Psalms 22:1-31, Jonah 1:1-3:4.

Chapter 22 ~ Monday

The Brightness and Glory of the Lord

T he sun was beginning to come up at the Cabin in the Way. Brenda and Mark made their way out of the bathroom to the kitchen table. An assortment of bagels and leftover donuts were assembled at the table on various paper plates and napkins. As Mark walked over to the table, Peter gave him a hug, a cup of coffee, and a half a donut. Then Peter asked his best friend, "Are you going to be alright?" Mark indicated that he was okay by giving a nod with his head while taking a sip of coffee. Both boys took a seat at the table with everyone else, as the first ray of sunshine beamed through the cabin. Then Mark said to Peter, "Thanks for being there for me; I really needed you this morning. You're a good friend."

Mark took his journal and set it on the table for everyone to see. He was no longer bound by secrecy and shame. Mark said to Peter while looking him in the eyes, "If it weren't for you asking me if there was anything else on my mind, I would have kept that secret bottled up inside for years to come or even worse..." Then Mark, looking at Brenda, gave her a smile, and as she looked into his eyes, a tear fell from her face. Clark said the group, "It's better to find out ahead of time that there's a problem rather than waiting until it's too late. It could turn into something that could quickly escalate and cause your life to spiral out of control." He indicated to Mark that acknowledging a problem existed was nothing to be ashamed of. All the kids walked over to Mark, reassuring him that they would be there for him in his time of need.

Shifting gears, Clark said, "Now we have to be out of here by 10:00, or the rangers are going to charge us for another day." So, at that point, the group began to pack their bags and clean up the cabin, getting it ready for someone else's use. Soon the bags were all packed, and the cabin was cleaned. All the campers were prepared for the upcoming hike back to the van.

Everyone's gear was stowed on the front porch, and they were ready to start their hike along the first marked trail. The group was standing outside when Clark said, "Are you guys ready for our group photo?" They all responded by getting into some kind of order. Becky said to Andrew, "Hey, I can't be in the back; I'm not tall enough." Andrew was teasing her by blocking her face from the camera. Mark was leaning against the front door of the cabin when an old rusty eye bolt that was screwed into the doorpost caught his eye. He asked Peter, "Dude, I wonder what that was for?" Peter answered, "There's no telling, but I'm sure it wasn't very important." As both boys looked at that old rusty eyebolt, they noticed it still had a rope tied to it, hanging down about six inches, and frayed at the end. It was a remnant of the rope which Jeffrey Maxwell used when he took his children to the outhouse during the blizzard of '52. You never know what God has used in the past that caused a problem or even a hardship, that years later would provide the needed components to fulfill the will of God in someone else's life (John 6:39-40).

The blizzard of '52 was a fierce storm. That rope was tied to the eye bolt fastened to the outhouse as the snow was falling profusely that Jeffrey had to use multiple times with his children. The two-and-a-half-day freak storm caused him and his children such hardship that he almost went mad at the council meeting following the storm. That very storm and its hardships caused Jeffrey to be sitting in the bathroom with Rodney when the comfort of Jesus Christ came over his life. Remember that Peter said, "I'm sure it wasn't very important." That old rusty eyebolt's value couldn't be measured, but it was one of the components in God's will. It led to the needed privacy for Mark to open up to Peter and Brenda early that morning. Because of the hardship on Jeffrey Maxwell and his children, he built that bathroom back in '52.

Click—went the camera shutter as the annual group photo of the Cabin in the Deep Dark Woods was just snapped, capturing the youth group from the Truth Valley Church. Someone from that group will be sure to notice one day when they are rummaging through the memories of that trip, the faded Edwardsville town motto above the door to the Cabin in the Way. That was what the children saw each day as they entered the School in the Way.

> Matthew 22:37-40 Jesus said to him," 'You shall love the LORD your God with all your heart, with all your soul, and with all your mind.' "This is the first and great commandment." And the second is like it: 'You shall love your neighbor as yourself.' "On these two commandments hang all the Law and the Prophets."

Everyone gathered along the stone wall in front of the cabin to begin their hike. But, Peter went back inside the cabin one last time, checking for items that he may have left behind. As Peter shut the door, a hooded man put his hand on Peter's shoulder. He said ever so kindly, "Peter, ever since I gave you the video camera, you have known that you would have to return it." At that, Peter faced him, with great fear, like the fear of God, he took the treasure chest out of his backpack and handed it to the hooded man. While the treasure chest was still in Peter's outstretched arms, the hooded man opened it and removed the video camera. He lifted his eyes to heaven with great reverence as the video camera vanished away, and Peter watched in utter amazement. The hooded man looked into Peter's eyes through the veil and said, "You can keep the treasure chest," pushing it into Peter's chest. Peter felt a great warmth flowing from the hooded man's hands, knowing deep down that this man had great authority and power that only comes from above. The hooded man turned to walk away, and Peter could see partially through the veil, the brightness and glory of the Lord on His face like that of an Angel. He knew that this hooded Man had protected him by veiling His face (Exodus 34:29-35). As the hooded Man left the cabin, He said to Peter, "I will come in to him and dine with him, and he with Me" (Revelation 3:20).

Peter closed the cabin door behind him and joined the others as they began their hike along the first marked trail that led to the cabin's parking lot. Peter turned around one more time to look at the Cabin in the Way. Mark sensed that something had happened moments ago. "What's going on, bro?" asked Mark. In detail, Peter explained what had just transpired with the hooded Man. As the two boys talked, they once again fell behind the others during the hike. Clark abruptly stopped without even looking back and said to the others, "Let me guess! Let me guess! Peter and Mark are way back there, right?" Jill put her hand in his and said, "Yes, but I think they're going to be alright this time." Peter and Mark managed to catch up while Peter told Mark about the last part of Revelation 3:20, saying, "Mark, I felt like the hooded man was a heavenly being. After this weekend, I'm going to live, so Jesus never has to knock on the door of my heart."

Peter and Mark continued to talk back-and-forth about that weekend. They ended up walking ahead of the group for the first time. Before long, they were the first ones to reach the parking lot where the church van was parked. Within a few minutes, most of the group was assembled around the van loading their gear in the back. But it was Brad and Daisy this time who fell behind and managed to hold up the group. They were deeply entrenched in a discussion. Brad was questioning his twin sister Daisy, about what she saw on the video camera that second time. It was while Jill was praying so deeply the night before when Daisy abruptly slammed the camera view screen shut.

Discussion Questions:

1) Can you think of a time in your life when you suspected a friend or a loved one had issues similar to the ones Mark was facing in his life? After Mark admitted his problems, bringing them to the surface, he took the first step to overcome them.

Can you think of any place in the Bible where this type of situation is discussed?

Answer: Luke 8:16-18, Ecclesiastes 12:13-14, Luke 12:1-3, Matthew 10:26, and Romans 2:11-16.

2) The power and authority that Peter felt from the hooded man while giving back the video camera were impressive. Can you think of a time when you were faced with a situation that you had no power to overcome? There are examples in the Bible that display the mighty power of God. Can you think of some of them?

Answer: Genesis 7:7-13, Joshua 10:12-14, and Luke 24:1-9.

3) The hooded man said the last part of Revelation 3:20 to Peter. What do you think about this verse in its entirety? Do you see it as a play on words when used to justify the use of the sinner's prayer, or do you see it as a warning to the individual and the church that there is a certain standard that Jesus is expecting from believers?

Scriptures: John 6:39-40, Matthew 22:37-40, Exodus 34:29-35, Revelation 3:20.

Discussion Question Scriptures: Luke 8:16-18, Ecclesiastes 12:13-14, Luke 12:1-3, Matthew 10:26, Romans 2:11-16, Genesis 7:7-13, Joshua 10:12-14, Luke 24:1-9, Revelation 3:20.

Chapter 23 ~ Monday

Eyes of Sin

Brad had been questioning his twin sister Daisy since they left the cabin that morning about what she saw on the video camera the night before. The two of them were standing in a small clearing just a short distance from the van out of earshot from the others while talking rather intently.

"Yes, that's exactly what happened," Daisy said to Brad. However, Brad responded by saying, "But Daisy, that just doesn't make any sense." "Brad, I'm telling you the truth, that's exactly what I saw. It was so vile and hideous, and the way it looked at me made my blood curdle," said Daisy once more, trying to get her older brother to understand what had troubled her so much. Brad, only seventeen minutes older, had always been overprotective of his twin sister. But, Daisy always responded with, "I let you go first because you were acting like a baby." Nonetheless, it was clear to Brad that his sister was noticeably shaken and disturbed by what she saw that second time on the video camera.

Suddenly a hooded man appeared to Brad and Daisy and joined their conversation. He said in a voice that sounded like a choir: "Daisy, what you saw on the video camera last night was something no one on earth had ever witnessed before. It is the great mystery of the Heavenly Father (John 3:1-21). It is the exact moment of conversion when the vile and hideousness of the flesh nature has been rejected by the heart, mind, and soul. You looked into the eyes of sin that prohibits someone from being born again. There is nothing on earth that despises God more than the sin nature at the exact moment of conversion." (John 3:8, John 12:23-26, Romans 8:12-17, John 11:25-26).

The hooded man continued: "Let me share with you what happened next, that you didn't see. The vileness that was Jill's very own nature died moments after you slammed the camera shut. What you missed was the beauty of the Holy Spirit descending on her like He did on Jesus when baptized in the Jordan River by John" (Mark 1:10). The hooded man paused and looked up to heaven for almost a full minute in worship and adoration to Christ the Lord. Everyone watched Brad and Daisy, wondering why they were just staring into the sky, no longer speaking to each other. "What are those two doing just standing there?" Lisa asked.

Then the hooded man said, "It was Jesus who died on the cross at Calvary and rose the third day so that all mankind may have access to His saving grace and mercy." The hooded man looked at Brad and Daisy and said: "Every one is tempted by the devil. When the Holy Spirit is received, the devil and Satan will be on the attack. He tempted Eve in the garden of Eden (Genesis 3:1-6). And, even Jesus was tempted by Satan in the wilderness for forty days (Mark 1:12-13). As Jesus was tempted, so also will Jill Williams be tempted. All mankind can overcome that temptation by the word of God."

> The hooded man continued: "Jesus said to Satan in the wilderness, 'It is written, people shall not live by bread alone, but by every word that proceeds from the mouth of God.' Jesus said a second time to him, 'It is written again, you shall not tempt the Lord your God.' Then Jesus said a final time to Satan, 'it is written, you shall worship the Lord your God and Him only you shall serve.' Then the devil left Him (Matthew 4:1-11). Jesus has provided a way out from temptation,

and that way is through the Holy Spirit and prayer. As God talks to you, He is writing His standards on your heart, and when this happens, the devil has no authority over your life."

And with that last word, the hooded man vanished in front of Brad and Daisy. Then the two of them joined the group in the van. They begin to share what transpired with the hooded man explaining how important it is to know the voice of the Holy Spirit to overcome the temptations that are sure to come.

As the church van began to leave the cabin parking lot, Clark abruptly slammed on the brakes as an Edwardsville fire engine screamed by with its red lights flashing, its siren blaring, and air horn blasting, getting his attention so that he stopped. As the fire truck raced by, Brad noticed that the fire engine said on its side: Edwardsville Volunteer Fire Department Engine No.1. Becky took that moment to look out the window, and she saw an old decrepit mailbox that seemed as if it should have been replaced over a decade ago. It said, 1224 Sandrock Creek Blvd., The Cabin in the Way.

Discussion Questions:

1) While reading John 3:8: Can you fully grasp how that a person is born again? It is a mystery, and it is hard to understand. It can best be explained that once an individual has been converted, they will look at things from a different perspective. Can you think of anyone that has had a change in their life? This may be indicative of having been covered by the blood of Jesus, converted from living a life of sin, and having received the Holy Spirit becoming born again?

2) Can you think of a place in the Bible where the Apostle Paul distinguishes between man's flesh nature and the spiritual nature of God?
Answer: Romans 2:25-29, Colossians 2:11-15.
Is there any place in the Old Testament where a similar discussion takes place?
Answer: Ezekiel 36:25-27, Zechariah 3:1-7.

3) The hooded man said, "It is the exact moment of conversion when the vile and hideousness of the flesh nature has been

rejected by the heart, mind, and soul." Thinking of that statement, answer the two questions below:

3a) Have you ever been transformed from serving the god of this world (who is the devil and Satan) to becoming a child of God?

3b) Do you remember a time in your life described in Question 3a?

Scriptures: John 3:1-21, John 3:8, John 12:23-26, Romans 8:12-17, John 11:25-26, Mark 1:10, Genesis 3:1-6, Mark 1:12-13, Matthew 4:11, Matthew 4:1-11.

Discussion Question Scriptures: John 3:8, Romans 2:25-29, Colossians 2:11-15, Ezekiel 36:25-27, Zechariah 3:1-7.

Chapter 24 ~ Monday

Contending for the Faith

J ill looked over at her husband with an intense stare and asked him, "Would you like me to drive now, Sir?!" At that moment, Clark realized that he had not been paying attention. He looked to his right and saw Jill's face, and out of the corner of his eye, in the distance, he could still see the fire truck with its red lights flashing, traveling down the road. Feeling somewhat chastised by Jill's question, he said to her, "No, I think I'm good now." Clark pulled the van onto the highway and began the six-hour drive back to the church.

In the back of the van, a discussion began about that incident in the cabin with the hooded man, just before their hike that morning. As Peter told the story, Brad said, "Wow, man, I can't believe you don't have the video camera anymore!" With a confidence that he had not possessed before this trip, Peter said, "I know, it's gone. I had to give it back to the hooded man this morning." Andrew said, "Having an insight into the spiritual realm would become a hindrance. Even the Pharisees and scribes wanted Jesus to give them a sign after they knew He had performed a miracle by healing a man with a deformed hand." (Matthew 12:9-14 & 38-39). And then Peter told the group how the hooded man spoke the third part of Revelation 3:20 to him that morning. Remembering the discussion about the scroll from Friday, Brad said, "That's the last part of the verse from the scroll." Peter began to share what the Holy Spirit had revealed to him about the three parts of Revelation 3:20.

> Peter said: "The first part of the verse, 'I stand at the door and knock,' indicates that Jesus is attempting to get our attention, as He is outside our temple. This may be yourself or your church; regardless, Jesus Christ is calling to everyone. The second part, 'If anyone hears My voice and opens the door.' Jesus is giving a promise to anyone who hears His voice, instructing them to open the door of their lives in faith. Once that door is opened, Jesus Christ will enter in with His Holy Spirit, thus fulfilling the third part. 'I will come in to him and dine with him, and he with Me.' It is in this third and final statement that Jesus will establish a relationship with that person, church, or nation. That final part of the verse is everlasting, and it is Jesus Christ who is leading the relationship. The promises of God to Abraham will follow as long as they continue to walk in the light and truth of the gospel of Jesus Christ. This is the beginning of a friendship between Jesus and the faithful believer." (Genesis 17:1-9, James 2:23-24, John 15:15).

It wasn't long after that discussion that almost everyone was asleep in the back of the van. Peter, however, was unable to sleep. His mind was deep in thought as he pondered a decision that he had made during that trip. It was one of those decisions that didn't seem right at the time, but he did it anyway, knowing all the while, deep down in his heart that it was wrong. Peter looked over at Mark, seeing that he had also fallen asleep. Peter began to think about a way to remedy the situation, knowing that it wouldn't be easy. As Peter contemplated the dilemma, he too was overcome by the hum of the tires as they met the pavement—only to be interrupted by an occasional bump in the road as the van continued to cruise down the highway. Shortly, Peter also fell asleep.

After a while, the van changed pitch as Clark slowed down, pulling into that same gas station with the mountain view. It was full sunshine and picturesque, and everyone had awakened, except for Mark. Clark once again told everyone to use the buddy system and to stick together. All the kids exited the van except Peter and Mark. Peter said, "Hey buddy, we're at the gas station, our next stop is the church, and that's a long way." Mark got the idea; he was still tired from waking up so early that same morning. As they got out of the van, Peter and Mark headed directly to the back of the gas station to take a last look at that beautiful mountain view.

As they walked around back and were looking at the mountain tops in the distance, another hooded man appeared behind them with his face veiled. He began to speak, with the voice of assurance, "Eyes sees you, Peter. Eyes sees you, Mark." This time the two boys had no fear of the hooded man, having a sense of comfort at his presence. Then the hooded man said, "Peter, you cannot give away a gift that God has given to you." At that, Peter and Mark knew what they must do. Mark took the clay jar out of his backpack and, with his arms extended, offered it to the hooded man. The hooded man removed the ancient scroll. He held it over his head, and it disappeared just like the video camera did earlier. Then looking directly at Peter, he said, "Peter, you were given a great responsibility during this trip to the Cabin in the Way. You handled the video camera and the ancient scroll very well and brought glory to God by your good works" (Matthew 5:13-16).

Then the hooded man, with eyes ablaze and the voice of promise, looked at Mark and said: "Mark, your friend Peter tried to give you his gift from God. But I have been sent to tell you that you will need to seek God for yourself by earnestly praying and contending for the faith. Then the gift of God will be given to you without measure. Seek the Lord your God with all your heart, soul, and mind having no other gods before Him." The hooded man handed the clay jar back to Mark to keep. Then he left Peter and Mark and disappeared into the mountain range before their very eyes. (Ephesians 2:8, Jude 3, John 3:34, Matthew 22:37-40).

Then Peter confessed to Mark, "I knew all along that I wasn't supposed to give you the ancient scroll, but I did it anyway." Mark knew Peter had always tried to help him along and that he was going to have to come to the truth of God on his own. Mark thought to himself, "The interpretation that Peter gave on Revelation 3:20 was intended for me. It's going to be a good starting point to find my way to God."

As the van got back on the road, Clark said to Jill, "Well, honey, that sure was an intense weekend if I must say so myself." "It certainly was," said Jill, with a tear streaming down her face. As Jill looked out the side window at the mountains, she repeated it in her head, "Yes, it certainly was!"

As the youth group made their final leg of the journey home, Mark began to think about his relationship with God or the lack thereof. He was deep in thought and oblivious to the conversations that were going on between the others. He began to review, in his mind, the events of that weekend.

Marks Thoughts:

Where is my life heading, and is there a blueprint being written on my heart with instructions directing me to the will of God? Is my foundation really built on the sand? Could I have the courage to build a relationship with God on the rock? What storms lay ahead for me? Will I be able to bear the devastation of those storms? Have I disregarded the wisdom of God in my dreams as foolishness and not felt the wind in my face as I walked into the storm? What form does the invitation of God come in? Have I become deaf to His calling? Will I ever decide to repent of lying to myself and hardening my heart? Have I shut myself in or shut myself out? Will I survive my selfishness? Will I ever be able to keep a family and protect them against the tricks of the devil? Will I be angry at God when my offering is not accepted? Can I hear God asking me, "Mark, why are you angry at Me for NOT accepting your sin?" Will the Lord continue to council me? Will sin be my ruler and demise? Am I a murderer? Could I kill my own friend? Whose blood am I accountable for? Should I desire to be my brother's keeper so that his blood is not upon my hands? Will my strength fail me before I seek the Lord? Am I forever stuck in the works of the flesh? Whenever I look behind me, will sin be at my heel? Whom will I seek to kill, lie to, or deceive? Am I but dust in the end? Will the smoke of my torment ascend forever? Will I ever be full of the fruit of the spirit?

With that last thought from Mark, the van pulled into the Church parking lot, where several cars had been patiently waiting for the returning campers. Soon, everyone was reunited, and they all said their final goodbyes. Shortly after that, Pastor James and Peter were taking Mark home. Mark's grandmother phoned Pastor James that morning and ask him to pick Mark up from the church, saying, "I just haven't been myself lately." Before anyone from that trip to the Cabin in the Deep Dark Woods fell asleep that night, they all remembered the move of God that happened at the Cabin in the Way.

Discussion Question:

1) Review the questions that Mark asked himself on the way back to the church (Mark's Thoughts). Try applying them to your own life.

Scriptures: {Matthew 12:9-14 & 38-39}, Revelation 3:20, Genesis 17:1-9, James 2:23-24, John 15:15, Matthew 5:13-16, Ephesians 2:8, Jude 3, John 3:34, Matthew 22:37-40.

Discussion Question Scriptures: none.

Chapter 25 ~ Years Later

The Cabin in the Way ~ A Summary

I want to share how everyone's lives were changed by being touched by the Spirit of God during that weekend so long ago at the Cabin in the Way.

Senior Pastor James Myers stepped down as pastor of the Truth Valley Church shortly after he repented of his sins and was born again. The Myers's took in Mark, and he lived with them until college. One day Pastor James took Peter and Mark out to lunch at the Old Horse Thief Hamburger Stand and let them order anything they wanted from the menu. The three of them had such a great time that they almost got kicked out of a restaurant that catered to horse thieves, not bad for an old charred pastor. Later, he said in his testimony: "Looking back on my time as a pastor, I realized I had taken that position as a profession and not a calling. It wasn't until I got myself right with God, and I was truly converted, that I started to hear the voice of the Holy Spirit. It was then I discovered my true calling was in writing, not preaching." As James later put it, "I had a lot of head knowledge and not much heart." Within a few months of stepping down as pastor, James got a call from the Daily Wind Newspaper and began his writing career. He wrote a weekly column on the Holy Spirit.

Stacy Myers stood by her husband in his conversion and the new job. She said: "It was a difficult time, but I always felt he had something missing in his life, and I prayed for him every day. I stood by him when godly sorrow took hold of his life. And I was by his side when he broke and poured his heart out before God in repentance, becoming born again. I will continue to pray for the Lord to lead and guide him through the trials and sufferings that are sure to come." After that, the Myers's were happier than ever. (II Corinthians 7:8-12, I Peter 5:10, Ezekiel 18:25-30, Acts 3:19-21).

It was sometime after James took the job at the Daily Wind Newspaper that his brother Chris read one of his columns. That particular column highlighted how people are supposed to renew the Spirit of God within themselves, according to Titus 3:4-5. After reading that article, Chris dedicated his life to Jesus Christ. Soon after, he received the Baptism of the Holy Spirit. James and his brother were never close until they came to know Jesus in spirit and truth. When the two of them got together, they would talk about Jesus or the Bible. This lifestyle was based upon the fact that the Holy Spirit had encompassed all aspects of their life. Whether sports, politics, or family, they always brought the conversation back to their savior, Jesus Christ.

Andrew received a call from his mother, urging him to get to the hospital right away. As he entered the hospital room, he saw his wife sitting up in her bed, and he said to her, "I can't believe I missed it. I just can't believe it!" His wife, Becky, said to him, "It's alright, honey. Our son was born an hour ago; let's call him Stephen."

Becky walked in dark places since her home life had not been ideal. She realized that the environment of her home was the dark places. Her mother drank a lot, and her father was nowhere to be found. The dark places that she walked through could be associated with the rocks and stones of Mark 4:5-6 & 16-17. Soon after the Cabin in the Way, those spiritual stones in her life caused Becky to dry up inside. It was as if she had to completely dry up spiritually, to fully recognize the joy she had experienced, while listening to Andrew give those Bible study lessons. They enabled Becky to have an enlightening moment, revealing how she was spiritually. It was when she saw Andrew at the supermarket that she instantly felt the dryness of her spirit. There in the frozen food aisle, Becky approached Andrew. That's when she realized the prophecy of her older-self had come full circle. They talked for almost an hour, and as Becky's ice cream melted, Andrew got up enough courage to ask her out for dinner. A few months before their wedding, she said to him, "I never forgot the lesson you gave on Hebrews 11:6 when you said, 'without faith, it is impossible to please God.'"

Clark realized when he looked Peter in the eyes that he had a special gift from God. It was on that last morning when Clark handed the video camera back to Peter while Brenda was still talking with Mark in the bathroom at the Cabin. Clark said to Peter: "I know God has His hand on you, and I also know why the Lord caused this video camera to be placed in your hands. You were strong enough to perform the duty that He laid out for you before the foundation of the world" (Ephesians 1:4). Peter was humbler than when the weekend had started. Peter looked up and said to Clark with tears streaming down his face: "Mr. Williams, sometimes in life, we are given a task that we know deep down in our heart we must complete. This was one of those times in my life. I knew if I didn't press hard to use the gift God had given me that I would have regretted it for the rest of my life." Clark took Peter's hand in his, and the two of them sat in silence for a few moments. It was one of those times when the presence of the Holy Spirit could be felt (Matthew 18:20).

Clark was stirred in his spirit when he had an experience like the one Jill had in the cabin on that Sunday night. He said, "I was truly converted, and I received the baptism of the Holy Spirit right there in my living room with my beautiful wife, Jill." Like Clark put it, "It's hard to be bitter at someone you call beautiful." He sure had a point there. (Acts 11:15-18, Acts 19:1-7, Romans 8:8-11, I Corinthians 12:13).

Clark's conversion happened when he and his wife were home together one evening. Clark began to review in his heart the events that occurred during that long weekend at the cabin. He started feeling his own sinfulness rising to the surface of his life. He realized he was living according to his own flesh nature, and the Spirit of God was far from him. He began to cry out to Jesus, knowing in his heart that he must become a friend of God and receive the Spirit of promise that Jesus talked about with His disciples (Acts 1:4-5). Then he cried out, saying, "Abba, Father, hear my cry and let me receive that Spirit of promise so that I can be called a friend of God." It was a great crying out, and many tears flowed. The kind of tears that not only flow from your eyes but also from your nose and mouth. It was uncontainable and a total surrender that could be described as simply: not the will of the flesh. Then Jill joined her husband, remembering her own emptying out of the flesh nature that happened at the cabin after Daisy witnessed Jill's sin nature, with the video camera, as her desires of the flesh were being put to death. That was when the Spirit of the living God entered in and became Lord of her life. Clark and Jill were water baptized shortly after being born again, following the example of the Lord Jesus. Jill and Clark began serving coffee and snacks at the Truth Valley Church Coffee Barn; since that time, the gossip has stopped, and the truth has been found. (Luke 3:21-22, Romans 8:12-17, Galatians 3:14, John 14:12-14, James 2:23, Ephesians 1:13-14, Isaiah 41:8).

When they got home from the Cabin in the Way, two packets were sitting on their dining room table from the Foreign Adoption Commission. They outlined the steps they would need to take if an adoption opportunity became available. It was Flippers, the cockatiel, who guarded those packets until Clark and Jill returned home. The Williams's have since adopted two children. The first was a boy from Cambodia named Sophal, who was three years old and a girl from Thailand named Deborah, who was eight. Several years after that, Jill gave birth to a baby boy, and they named him Daniel after the late Pastor Edwards. Love has multiplied and is back on the throne, and they are a happy family.

Jill remembered feeling a pricking in her heart that day at the Coffee Barn. It was when she and Clark were about to go into the main sanctuary for the worship session. It was then that she noticed the two Summers sisters were sitting behind them. She could never justify the words she spoke against their mother and never found the courage to ask for forgiveness. Jill could not stop gossiping until the Holy Spirit brought about conviction. He enabled her to approach Sara one afternoon at her home, and the two women talked in the privacy of Sara's bedroom. Sara not only opened her home to Jill but also her heart. Forgiveness is powerful.

Jill began to live a life of holiness; she was tempted as the devil wanted nothing more than to sift her like wheat. She was able to overcome that temptation—well, not all on her own. It was through her daily reading of the Bible, her prayer life, and of course, her mentor Sara.

Lisa sought out repentance that second day in the cabin and received Jesus Christ as her personal savior. Jesus helped her to see herself as she really was, which set in motion the events that led to her conversion that same day. Even after pouring her heart out and repenting, Lisa still held a hardness towards Jill, until she heard Clark say that Jill was a beautiful woman. That helped Lisa consider that Jill deserved to have someone say to her, "Mrs. Williams, you know we all love you." This was the catalyst that led Jill to break and become humble in the spirit that night.

Sara married her coworker that she gave the flowers to, whose wife had passed away. Sara's new husband, Zackery Kelley, was the president of the company that Sara had worked for since Rickey passed away. The Summers's no longer lived in their government-assisted apartment. Brenda, Brad, Daisy, and Lisa all lived with their mother and her new husband, along with his daughter Jackie, in a new two-story house.

Pastor Melvin Baldwin, from Southland Bible College, became the Senior Pastor at the Truth Valley Church. Associate Pastor Arron Carpenter was a successful businessman who funded many programs at the church and the community.

Pastor Baldwin took full advantage of the stories and testimonies that came out of the cabin and pressed the church to open the door for revival, which led to countless conversions. It was that type of revival that affected their church and other churches in the community. One part of that revival was that multiple churches crossed their inviable boundaries and founded the Home Bible Study Association. This was based on Hebrews 10:25, where the author encouraged the body of Christ to meet together. Those meetings of the HBSA were straightforward. They were designed to get people reading their Bibles in small groups. It was in the establishment of these small groups that new leaders emerged. And it wasn't long before these groups began to hunger for more knowledge of God through the word. One such method for someone to follow as a new believer was the chain reference Bible study.

Chain Reference Bible Study:

This is the three-step process of conducting a chain reference Bible study, utilizing a center column reference Bible.

Step 1: Pick any Bible verse that interests you. For example, John 3:16, then read and discuss in a group.

Step 2: Look in the center column for a cross-reference to that verse. Select Romans 5:8, then read, and discuss in a group.

Step 3: Continue the process until time expires. Sample verses: John 3:16, Romans 5:8, I John 4:10, Luke 18:13, Romans 3:25.

This type of study took off rather quickly since there was virtually no preparation time required, and most people tend to be extremely busy. Many people who used this type of study would comment that at some point in the meeting, the Holy Spirit would show up (Matthew 18:20).

Mark Phillips moved in with the Myers's after his grandmother was unable to care for him. After the incident in the bathroom at the cabin, Mark only thought about suicide twice. Both times, he remembered the eyes of Brenda, and the feeling passed rather quickly. He was able to get the professional help he needed, and no longer thought about taking his own life. He always credited the quick thinking of Brenda and the *Instruction to the Way of Life Journal* (Found in Appendix D). Peter was a great accountability partner. Mark had called him several times when he had the urge to look at pornography, but that also passed. Mark realized he had not always been truthful, especially when he and Peter were questioned about the treasure chest and the ancient scroll. That was until listening to Associate Pastor Arron Carpenter's message on truth one Sunday morning. Pastor Carpenter said, "Whenever a small lie is concealed and hidden in truth, it is still a lie as no truth can contain or hide a lie." Pastor Carpenter went on to preach that day on Revelation 21:8. Pastor Carpenter said, "All liars will have their part in the lake of fire." Soon after that message, Mark turned his life over to God by repenting of his self-centeredness, his flesh nature, and all the lies that he had told over the years. Mark read his Bible every day for twenty to thirty minutes and began a prayer life. His prayer life wasn't perfect; however, he kept a prayer journal, and when he failed to pray for a few days or even a week, he just picked back up where he left off and continued to talk to Jesus.

Gertrude Phillips, Mark's grandmother, had to be placed in a care center when she was unable to care for herself or Mark because Alzheimer's got the best of her. She had been a believer for many years, and God helped her persevere through life. She passed away soon after being admitted to the care center, but not until she discovered her prayers had been answered; her grandson Mark had been born again.

When I was a young man, Peter Myers would tell me the stories that happened at the Cabin in the Way. Years later, he gave me the treasure chest that the hooded man let him keep. Some years after that trip to the Cabin in the Way, Peter wrote the book, *The Cabin in the Deep Dark Woods,* quickly becoming a number one bestseller. After Peter published his book, it was discovered that similar events had happened at the Cabin in the Way. Numerous letters were sent to him describing events similar to those found in his book—other letters gave testimonies of events that were described as remarkable, astonishing, and amazing. Peter and

Mark are still best friends. My name is Alex Myers, and I am the son of Peter Myers, the famous author and speaker.

Discussion Questions: none.

Scriptures: II Corinthians 7:8-12, I Peter 5:10, Ezekiel 18:25-30, Acts 3:19-21, Titus 3:4-5, {Mark 4:5-6 & 16-17}, Hebrews 11:6, Ephesians 1:4, Matthew 18:20, Acts 11:15-18, Acts 19:1-7, Romans 8:8-11, I Corinthians 12:13, Acts 1:4-5, Luke 3:21-22, Romans 8:12-17, Galatians 3:14, John 14:12-14, James 2:23, Ephesians 1:13-14, Isaiah 41:8, Hebrews 10:25, John 3:16, Romans 5:8, I John 4:10, Luke 18:13, Romans 3:25, Matthew 18:20, Revelation 21:8.

Chapter 26 ~ Twenty Years Later

The Cabin in the Deep Dark Woods ~ Epilogue

As the Cub Scouts pulled into the cabin's parking lot, they saw a mailbox lying on the ground with the address 1224 Sandrock Creek Blvd., which should have been replaced long ago. As the scouts disembarked from the van, the scout leader, a rather large man named Paul Armstrong, said to the boys, "Okay, boys listen up, grab your backpacks, we're going to take the first marked trail to the cabin." As they made their way along the trail, it was a relatively uneventful hike through some beautiful countryside. The sky was hinting that there may be a wet weekend ahead. Paul mentioned to his assistant scout leader, Wade Blanton, "I sure hope we can keep these boys entertained this weekend; it looks like we may be cooped up inside." As the boys and the scout leaders arrived at the cabin, there was an expectation of an amazing weekend ahead. There were five boys and two scout leaders in all. This was no ordinary group of kids as they all had special needs.

It was Matthew Preston who was the first boy to burst through the front door of the Cabin in the Way. With his backpack still on, flinging side to side, he ran throwing it on the first bed he came across. He continued to the kitchen without even stopping, there he noticed a book was sitting on the corner of the table. He grabbed the book and then ran back to the front door. He tripped with one shoe untied, falling flat on the hardwood floor, sliding headfirst into his scout leader's feet. Matthew looked up at the big man, excited at finding the book, hardly able to speak. Matthew held it up in the air as if he had just caught the last out of the World Series. Paul bent down, and with both hands, he picked Matthew up off the ground and sat him on a chair, tying his shoe one more time. He said with a kind gentle voice, "Hey, what have you got there, buddy." He read to Matthew from the front cover of the book, *"The Cabin in the Deep Dark Woods, written by Peter Myers."* Paul Armstrong had always been a good man, but he had never given any thought to the Lord Jesus Christ. And while Paul still held the book in his hand, the prayer of Daniel Edwards made its way boldly before the Throne of Grace, "My dearest Lord and Heavenly Father…

Discussion Questions:

1) Have you ever turned your life over to Jesus Christ through repentance? Was your repentance accompanied by a confession of your sins? Has that action produced holiness?

2) What scriptures can you think of that represent Jesus as the way to salvation?
   Answer: John 10:7-9, John 14:6, Ephesians 2:14-18, and Hebrews 10:19-25.

Scripture Section: John 3:16 "For this is how God loved the world: He gave his one and only Son, so that everyone who believes in him will not perish but have eternal life [NLT].

The Lords Supper: I Corinthians 11:23-26.

Scriptures: none.

Discussion Question Scriptures: See Discussion Question 2.

Thank You from the Author

Thank you for purchasing *The Cabin in the Deep Dark Woods*. As a special gift I would like to send you a free PDF of *The Minister of the Holy Spirit*, a 90-day study of the scriptures. I like to call it the Holy Spirit on training wheels. Just send an email to:
TheCabin@turnifyouwill.org
TheCabinInTheDeepDarkWoods.com
I hope you enjoyed your stay at the Cabin in the Deep Dark Woods. Please be sure to visit again when the next book is published—*The Spirit and the Bride.*
Thank you
Tim Barker

Appendix A ~ From Chapter 1

Depart From Me

Note: Italics are utilized to indicate scripture.

I t must be clear who Jesus was speaking to in Matthew 7:21-23. From Chapter 1: 'CLICK' went the radio dial as Pastor James turned it off. Who may these people be…? They are the ones who thought they were saved but were never truly converted in the first place. *Matthew 7:21 "Not everyone who says to Me, 'Lord, Lord,' shall enter the kingdom of heaven, but he who does the will of My Father in heaven. (22) "Many will say to Me in that day, 'Lord, Lord, have we not prophesied in Your name, cast out demons in Your name, and done many wonders in Your name?' (23) "And then I will declare to them, 'I never knew you; depart from Me, you who practice lawlessness!'* From this passage, there will be people, even members of local churches, who will one day stand before Jesus Christ and have those horrible words spoken to them, DEPART FROM ME.

The Holy Spirit asked me one morning, "What's the strong epistle?" I searched the internet for the strong epistle wanting to give an answer. I couldn't find anything to support His question. So, I came up with a grading sheet that would measure the epistles for strength based on the characteristics of the seven Spirits of God found in Isaiah 11:2. And for the following: *is profitable for doctrine, for reproof, for correction, for instruction in righteousness*—from II Timothy 3:16. Of all the epistles that I completed, Titus had the highest rating, but that wasn't what the Holy Spirit was after. There's one epistle not found in the Bible; it's the one being written on the heart of the believer by the Holy Spirit. This epistle is the strongest of all. Jesus said in John 11:25, *Jesus said to her," I am the resurrection and the life. He who believes in Me, though he may die, he shall live. 26" And whoever lives and believes in Me shall never die."* **If Jesus Christ, through the Holy Spirit, is not writing His standards on your heart, then you may be one of those people who will hear those horrible words: DEPART FROM ME.**

It's not as hard as you may imagine avoiding condemnation; however, there is more to it than just saying a little prayer and going on with your day. After all, how many people said a sinners prayer and were or will be told on their judgment day—DEPART FROM ME? Are you basing your eternal salvation (eternal security) on a prayer that you said once or twice, **or are you basing your salvation on EVERY WORD that Jesus said?** (Acts 17:11). Thus, avoiding the words—DEPART FROM ME— is a theme of this book. The words that you want to hear from Jesus are—WELL DONE, GOOD AND FAITHFUL SERVANT—Matthew 25:14-30.

From the following scriptures, I will highlight how God wants to guide all people, by his will, into His kingdom (John 6:39-40). The Apostle Paul warned that some acts or actions will prohibit people from entering God's kingdom. "*...that those who practice such things **will not** inherit the kingdom of God*" (Galatians 5:21). These acts are referred to as *works of the flesh*. The passages of Matthew 7:21-23 & Galatians 5:19-21 are warnings in contrast to John 3:1-10, where Jesus tells Nicodemus that he must be born again to enter the kingdom of God. In John 3, Jesus tells the reader that they must do something to enter God's kingdom. They must be born again, whereas, in the Matthew and Galatians passages, the authors discuss issues that will prohibit individuals from entering God's Kingdom. Then there is the how. How to be converted? Jesus declared in Mark 1:14-15 that all people are to repent, and believe in the gospel. Jesus further explains that everyone is to feed from Him spiritually. *John 6:27 "Do not labor for the food which perishes, but for the food which endures to everlasting life, which the Son of Man will give you, because God the Father has set His seal on Him."*

Therefore, eating from the Son of Man (Jesus) is a solution to a problem that occurred in Genesis 3:6; *So when the woman saw that the tree was good for food, that it was pleasant to the eyes, and a tree desirable to make one wise, she took of its fruit and ate. She also gave to her husband with her, and he ate.* One reason people are not able to take full advantage of the gospel message of Jesus Christ is they don't fully grasp that feeding from the Son of Man (Jesus Christ) is a prayer life. See also John 15:1-8.

The event of Genesis 3:6, when Eve was tempted in the garden of Eden, she ate the fruit the tree of the knowledge of good and evil. Hence, [*the tree of the knowledge*]. The result of that knowledge was death. The fruit/works of that knowledge are listed in Galatians 5:19-21, and they are in direct contrast to the fruit of the Spirit. Jesus said in John 3:6, *"That which is born of the flesh is flesh, and that which is born of the Spirit is spirit.* In Galatians 5:22, the amplified version brackets the meaning of *the fruit of the Spirit* as **[the result of His presence within us]**. Therefore, the result of God's presence within us is life. Jesus overcame His temptation in the wilderness by professing that *Man shall not live by bread alone, but by every word that proceeds from the mouth of God (Matthew 4:4).* Whereas, the result of Satan's presence within us is death. *"but of the tree of the knowledge of good and evil you shall not eat, for in the day that you eat of it you shall surely die (Genesis 2:17).*

The serpent is expanded on later in Revelation 20:2; *he laid hold of the dragon, that serpent of old, who is the Devil and Satan, and bound him for a thousand years.* A person is either feeding on the fruit of Jesus Christ, which is life, or feeding on the fruit of that serpent of old, who is the Devil and Satan, which is death. Therefore, there are two natures of man. The first is the flesh nature, and this is unto death, found in Matthew 7:21-23. The second is life in the Son of Man (Jesus Christ), located in John 6:27, *"Do not labor for the food which perishes, but for the food which endures to everlasting life, which the Son of Man will give you, because God the Father has set His seal on Him."*

We must continually feed on the Son of Man—Jesus Christ, and doing so is a prayer life. Paul says in II Timothy 1:3, *I thank God, whom I serve with a pure conscience, as my forefathers did, as without ceasing I remember you in my prayers night and day.* It is this prayer life and feeding on Jesus that is the key to entering into the kingdom of God. It's through prayer and reading the Bible that a true convert is instructed on the will of the Father. See Matthew 7:21 (*"Not everyone who says to Me, 'Lord, Lord,' shall enter the kingdom of heaven, **but he who does the will of My Father in heaven.***). Allowing Jesus to be Lord of one's life is denying that serpent of old, the Devil and Satan, any authority by following the Holy Spirit's guidance, thus fulfilling the will of the Father.

I draw strength From II Corinthians 3:1-6, that the Holy Spirit is giving instruction to the saving of the soul, so the will of the Father is accomplished in each person (John 6:39-40). Jesus Christ died on the cross so that all may come to the saving knowledge of the Father. However, it is up to each individual to follow that teaching and continue in the way the Lord instructs. *II Corinthians 3:3 clearly you are an epistle of Christ, ministered by us, written not with ink but by the Spirit of the living God, not on tablets of stone but on tablets of flesh, that is, of the heart.* Are you allowing God to write on your heart? Or have you hardened your heart through the works of the flesh? Thus, conforming to *that serpent of old, who is the Devil and Satan*? (Revelation 20.2). See Zechariah 3:1-7, the vision of the high priest.

Galatians 5:16-26: This passage starts off in vs. 16, saying, *"walk in the Spirit."* It is this walking in the spirit that denies the flesh authority enhancing spiritual growth or II Corinthians 3:3's ability for the Holy Spirit to guide all who are His in the way of truth by instructing His people throughout their day. Take the warning of Matthew 7:21-23 seriously as the devil wants to sift you like wheat. (Luke 22:31-34, Romans 2:1-16).

Genesis 4:1-8: The key verse in this passage is vs. 7, *"If you do well, will you not be accepted? And if you do not do well, sin lies at the door. And its desire is for you, but you should rule over it."* God was talking to Cain about the condition of his heart. In vs. 8, sin got the upper hand, and he killed his brother Abel. There is no joy in the Spirit with murder, much less the other works of the flesh. Take selfish ambitions; that's not close to murder, but it's a work of the flesh. The Bible says that those who practice selfish ambitions will not inherit the kingdom of God. All the works of the flesh in Galatians 5:19-21 are followed with: *that those who practice such things will not inherit the kingdom of God.* Again, I must ask the question: Who may these people be…? I sure don't want to be one of them, and I'm sure you don't either. The end result of not inheriting the kingdom of God is an eternity in the lake of fire, which is the second death (Revelation 21:7-8).

Ezekiel 36:25-27: Who may these people be…? Not the ones the Lord cleanses from all their filthiness with the clean water. Not the ones that the Lord gave a new heart and a new spirit. Not the ones the Lord causes to walk in His statutes keeping His judgments by doing them. There are no works of the flesh in that passage. So, who may these people be? Not those of Ezekiel 36:25-27. To enter into salvation, it must be understood that one of the first steps is to seek repentance from the Lord. This was made evident in Mark 1:14-15, when Jesus said, "Repent, and believe in the gospel." Read Psalms 51:1-17 and review Chapter 11 of this book—A Psalm of Repentance.

On the sinner's prayer: have you ever considered the passage from Hebrews 4:12; *For the word of God is living and powerful, and sharper than any two-edged sword, piercing even to the division of soul and spirit, and of joints and marrow, and is a discerner of the thoughts and intents of the heart.* Jesus is a discerner of the thoughts and intents of the heart. That means every sinner's prayer went before God and was discerned whether or not it was sincere. There are also passages in the Bible where the individual being saved didn't speak. For example, the woman of Luke 7:36-50 never spoke a word in that passage, yet Jesus proclaimed that her faith had saved her (From chapter 6—the Church Bulletin). This means that salvation is a Man, not a prayer. It's okay to say a prayer, but remember, the One to whom you are praying is also the One who grants your salvation. (Hebrews 5:9, Hebrews 12:2, Psalms 68:18-20, Isaiah 45:22, Acts 4:12, Romans 12:1-2, Psalms 34:18, II Kings 22:18-19, Isaiah 57:15, Luke 18:9-14).

Discussion Questions:
1) Have you ever thought about whom may these people be of Matthew 7:21-23? Would you like to know if you are one of them now rather than later?
2) When the Spirit of God moved upon the face of the waters, the waters were affected. What effect does the Spirit of God have on your life? Genesis 1:2 [KJV]

Scriptures: Matthew 7:21-23, Isaiah 11:2, II Timothy 3:16, John 11:25-26, Acts 17:11, Matthew 25:14-30, John 6:39-40, John 3:1-10, Mark 1:14-15, John 6:27, Genesis 3:6, John 15:1-8, John 3:6, Galatians 5:22 [AMP], Matthew 4:4, Genesis 2:17, Revelation 20:2, John 6:27, II Timothy 1:3, II Corinthians 3:1-6, Zechariah 3:1-7, Galatians 5:16-26, Luke 22:31-34, Romans 2:1-16, Genesis 4:1-8, Revelation 21:7-8, Ezekiel 36:25-27, Mark 1:14-15, Psalms 51:1-17, Hebrews 4:12, Luke 7:36-50, Hebrews 5:9, Hebrews 12:2, Psalms 68:18-20, Isaiah 45:22, Acts 4:12, Romans 12:1-2, Psalms 34:18, II Kings 22:18-19, Isaiah 57:15, Luke 18:9-14.

Discussion Question Scriptures: Matthew 7:21-23, Genesis 1:2.

Appendix B ~ From Chapter 3

Without Faith

Note: Italics are utilized to indicate scripture.

From Chapter 3 where Andrew said, "Today's Bible lesson is from Hebrews 11:6, without faith it is impossible to please God." This is the remainder of that lesson. *Hebrews 11:6 But without faith it is impossible to please Him, for he who comes to God must believe that He is, and that He is a rewarder of those who diligently seek Him.* This verse emphasizes that EVERYONE MUST BELIEVE that God is. **From the Strong's Greek rendering [God is] means I exist.** Therefore, to have faith in God, each person must believe that God actually exists. *Habakkuk 2:4 but the just shall live by his faith.* (Parallel passages: Galatians 3:11, Hebrews 10:38, Romans 1:17). To be faithful, one must believe that God exists and that He can perform what He said He will do. (Romans 4:20-21, Galatians 5:22-23). *Ephesians 2:8-9 For by grace you have been saved through faith, and that not of yourselves; it is the gift of God, ⁹not of works, lest anyone should boast.*

Jesus was in a boat with His disciples in Matthew 8:23, *Now when He got into a boat, His disciples followed Him.* *[24]And suddenly a great tempest arose on the sea, so that the boat was covered with the waves. But He was asleep.* *[25]Then His disciples came to Him and awoke Him, saying, "Lord, save us! We are perishing!"* *[26]But He said to them," Why are you fearful, O you of little faith?" Then He arose and rebuked the winds and the sea, and there was a great calm.* *[27]So the men marveled, saying, "Who can this be, that even the winds and the sea obey Him?"*

When Jesus was in that boat, He said to His disciples, *"O you of little faith"* (Matthew 8:26). This was in contrast to the events that transpired at the outpouring of the Holy Spirit in Acts 2:1-47, the lame man healed in Acts 3:1-26, and Tabitha raised from the dead in Acts 9:36-43. Those are some examples of the "just shall live by faith." There are more in the Bible if you care to search them out.

Having faith that God exists is important; however, after someone believes and has faith, it is important to know that Jesus Christ is our advocate with the Father. *I John 2:1 My little children, these things I write to you, so that you may not sin. And if anyone sins, we have an Advocate with the Father, Jesus Christ the righteous. 2 And He Himself is the propitiation for our sins, and not for ours only but also for the whole world.* Jesus is the propitiation, and He covered the sins of the sinner with His blood by the sacrifice that He made on the cross (Romans 3:25).

In conclusion, I refer to Matthew 7:21-23. In this passage, Jesus sends a warning to everyone who is betting their eternity on a one or two-minute prayer, where no tears were shed, no fear of God was felt, and no godly sorrow was presented in repentance. "Depart from Me, I never knew you." As I try to understand the depth of that statement, I am reminded that it is Jesus who will say it. Ask yourself: "How would I feel if I were one of those people, who at the judgment heard those words, just as Lisa did in chapter 4 when Jesus said to her, *'Assuredly, I say to you, I do not know you.'"*

How would you feel if while in a boat, you were hit by a wave and fell into the lake's frigid water? All the while, no one from the boat knew you had fallen into the water. Transition your thoughts: That frigid lake is the lake of fire. You have been cast into it by Jesus, because He did not know you since you never repented of your sins and accepted Him as your savior. From that point forward, you are destined to spend your eternity in the torments of the flames of the fire. Avoiding those words, **DEPART FROM ME,** has been one theme of this book. How were you saved? Was it a simple prayer? There's a reason that another word for being saved is conversion. With any conversion, a change must occur, or else there wasn't a conversion in the first place. This may be an excellent time to prove to yourself whether you were truly saved (II Timothy 2:15).

Another theme of this book is Revelation 3:20, where Jesus is standing at the door and knocking. Just asking Jesus to come into your heart is not necessarily the same as Titus 3:5, *not by works of righteousness which we have done, but according to His mercy He saved us, through the washing of regeneration and renewing of the Holy Spirit.* In John 20:19-23, Jesus entered a room where His disciples had assembled behind closed doors. Not only were the doors closed, but most commentaries support that they were also locked because the disciples feared persecution by the Jewish authority. Jesus entered that room with the doors being locked because His disciples knew His voice and were His followers. Then Jesus greeted them with one of the fruits of the Spirit saying, *"Peace be with you,"* saying it twice in the passage (vs. 19 & 21). The central idea was that the locked door didn't stop Jesus from fellowshipping with His disciples. Jesus didn't knock because He was already in a relationship with them. This is the same in a family; a wife doesn't knock on the door when she gets home because her husband loves her, and she knows it. However, if that same wife had to knock before she entered her home, there is a problem with that relationship. Knowing the disciples were grieved at His death, Jesus made His resurrection know to them by His manifestation. He knew His disciples would receive Him and be full of joy at His presence. Then Jesus breathed on them and said, "Receive the Holy Spirit."

In John 3:1-10, Nicodemus came to Jesus and asked about the new birth. If being born again were as simple as "saying a little prayer," Jesus might have said to Nicodemus, "Just repeat after Me and say this prayer of salvation," or He could have said, "Just ask Me to come into your heart." But Jesus didn't do that. Instead, he gave Nicodemus, a teacher of Israel, a lesson on the subject of being born again. If you are never born again, how will you avoid hearing the words "DEPART FROM ME?" What is your faith based on, and what will Jesus say to you when you stand before Him at the judgment?

Discussion Question:

1) If you could read the label of your heart as Jesus can, what would you find on your list of ingredients? Now think about a cake mix where the only requirement is to add water. Reading the label, the most prevalent ingredients would be listed first, such as flour, sugar, and baking soda. However, if you discovered that one of the ingredients was mercury, you would throw that box of cake mix into the trash as mercury is poisonous. Now back to your label: if Jesus were to pick you up and read the label of your heart, would He find goodness, love, joy, peace, self-control, and faithfulness as your primary ingredients, or would He find adultery, selfish ambitions, fornication, idolatry, hatred, or envy? Which box of you would Jesus keep in His kingdom, and which box would he cast into outer darkness? You are what's inside!

Scriptures: Hebrews 11:6, Habakkuk 2:4, Galatians 3:11, Hebrews 10:38, Romans 1:17, Romans 4:20-21, Galatians 5:22-23. Ephesians 2:8-9, Matthew 8:23-27, Acts 2:1-47, Acts 3:1-26, Acts 9:36-43, I John 2:1-2, Romans 3:25, Matthew

7:21-23, II Timothy 2:15, Revelation 3:20, Titus 3:5, John 20:19-23, John 3:1-10.

Discussion Question Scriptures: none.

Special Note: During the editing of this Faith Appendix B, I was actively praying for my 82 years old dad, who was having shortness of breath. The next day he was diagnosed with bilateral pulmonary embolism. This was a week after suffering a heart attack. Sometimes in life, the only thing that a person has is a little faith, so use your faith and let it grow. He is home and getting stronger every day. You never know when you will pray a loved one through two major life-threatening events.

Appendix C ~ From Chapter 9

Salvation a Measurable Objective ~ Study to Show Yourself Approved

Note: Italics are utilized to indicate scripture.

B*e diligent to present yourself approved to God, a worker who does not need to be ashamed, rightly dividing the word of truth (II Timothy 2:15).* In this verse, there are two elements. The first is a commission to get involved in studying the written word of God, which is the Bible. The second is to let God, through the Holy Spirit, reveal that same word to your heart, showing you what in your life is of God and what is not of God's nature.

Study to show yourself approved unto God: get involved in studying the written word of God. In Acts 17:11, there was a group of people who got involved in God's word daily, determined to prove to themselves that the words contained therein were really the words of God. The result of that "studying of the word" was that many believed upon the Lord Jesus (Acts 17:12). Then in I Thessalonians 2:4, Paul makes the statement: *But as we have been approved by God to be entrusted with the gospel, even so we speak, not as pleasing men, but God who tests our hearts.* Signifying that it is the Lord that speaks to all of us in our own spirit enabling each individual to feel the pressing authority of God on their hearts. This is further expanded in Psalms 44:21, *Would not God search this out? For He knows the secrets of the heart.* We can keep nothing from God as he knows all things. Let us walk worthy of the calling that Jesus Christ has placed on our lives (Ephesians 4:1). See also Psalms 139:1-24, Jeremiah 17:10, Hebrews 4:11-13.

Rightly dividing the word of truth: in II Corinthians 4:1-6, Paul states, *"⁴whose minds the god of this age has blinded, who do not believe."* This signifies that while living in the flesh nature, the things of God, the heavenly things have little to no value to an unbeliever. In John 3:6, Jesus distinguishes between the flesh nature and the spirit. *⁶" That which is born of the flesh is flesh, and that which is born of the Spirit is spirit.*

In Hebrews 5:12-14, there is a graduating scale of maturity in being a believer by going from the milk to the solid food of maturity; this gives way to the discernment of good and evil. Paul stated in Acts 26:18, *'to open their eyes, in order to turn them from darkness to light, and from the power of Satan to God, that they may receive forgiveness of sins and an inheritance among those who are sanctified by faith in Me.'*

Salvation is so critical that each person must spend time in God's word, making the decision based upon the Bible, whether they were truly saved or just living a lie. It would be better to find out now, by studying the Bible, rather than later, having Jesus say on judgment day "Depart from Me." You choose; which is the better time to find out the truth about yourself?!

Discussion Questions:
1) What will Jesus say to you on judgment day?
2) You choose; when is the better time to find out the truth about yourself?

Scriptures: II Timothy 2:15, Acts 17:11-12, I Thessalonians 2:4, Psalms 44:21, Ephesians 4:1, Psalms 139:1-24, Jeremiah 17:10, Hebrews 4:11-13, II Corinthians 4:1-6, John 3:6, Hebrews 5:12-14, Acts 26:18.

Appendix D ~ From Chapter 20

Suicide Journal ~ Instruction to the Way of Life

Note: Italics are utilized to indicate scripture.

The goal of the Suicide Journal Instruction to the Way of Life, is to extend the life of a desperate person by five days, by journaling their feelings and reading their responses on subsequent days of the journal process.

This Journal Is A Three-Step Process

Step one: admit to yourself that you have suicidal thoughts.

Step two: get a pen and paper. Write on anything that you can, even the wall or the mirror.

Step three: write down your thoughts on paper and answer question 1, question 2, and question 3.

Question 1. To be asked on journal day one. Can I wait until tomorrow to take my life?

Question 2. To be asked on journal day two through four. Upon reading my journal notes from yesterday, is my situation any less desperate?

Question 3. To be asked on journal day five. Upon review of my journal notes: is there an improvement in my will to live? And is there a glimmer of hope that my life has value?

Further instruction of the process: Your life has value. Life is what you make of it. What you put into it is the very thing that you get out of it. *John 15:22 [KJV] If I had not come and spoken unto them, they had not had sin: but now they have no cloak for their sin.* In this verse, Jesus speaks of a cloak or a hiding place. A cloak is something that conceals or hides. The fact that you have gotten this far in the Suicide Journal shows you have become honest with yourself. You have removed the cloak, your hiding place, that the only answer to your problem is suicide. There must be another answer to the question: "Should I take my own life today?"

The first question that needs to be asked: "Is there any value to my life?" **The second question is:** "Can I add value to my life?" **The answer to question one must be YES.** All life comes from God, and that alone **QUALIFIES YOU AS VALUABLE. The answer to question two must also be YES.** Adding value to your life is a daily process. You are the only one who can do this. You must understand that your thoughts are trying to kill you, and this is not of God. Mankind was created in God's Own image, and any opinion contrary to that is not of God. If while asking yourself, is there a glimmer of hope that my life has value and you said no, then you must understand that Jesus loves you anyway. Jesus also went to the cross and died for you. Cry out to God in your darkest hour, and He will hear your cry. Understandably, you may not be able to see tomorrow as a new day, but the love of God is everlasting. I hope this helps as no one but Jesus can fully understand your situation and have an answer to help you overcome your darkest hour. Seek Jesus, and you will find Him. Ask Jesus, and He will comfort you. Pray to Jesus, and He will hear you. When you are talking to Jesus, don't be afraid to pour your heart out and let your tears flow like a river. Jesus loves you.

John 1:1 In the beginning was the Word, and the Word was with God, and the Word was God.

John 6:57 "As the living Father sent Me, and I live because of the Father, so he who feeds on Me will live because of Me.

Suicide Journal Instructions

DAY ONE

Question 1. Can I wait until tomorrow to take my life? This answer will have to come from the heart, and a NO answer must be dismissed. You must be strong and say, "YES, I CAN LIVE ANOTHER DAY."

DAY TWO

Question 2. Upon reading my journal notes from yesterday, is my situation any less desperate? Your life must not be as hopeless on day two as it was on day one because you made it through the night. What did you write in your journal yesterday? Please read it and re-read it; you are the author. Rebuild your life based on the value that you have found between day one and day two.

DAY THREE

Continue to expand your thoughts and be honest with yourself. A big part of getting rid of suicidal thoughts is to be honest with yourself. If you tell yourself that you have no value long enough, eventually you will start to believe it. Truth begins within and expands to the outside in the form of value. Self-value and God are the cure to suicidal thoughts.

DAY FOUR

This is a reinforcement of day three. If you are on day four, then you have added four days of value to your life.

DAY FIVE

Question 3. To be asked on journal day five. Upon review of my journal notes, is there an improvement in my will to live? And is there a glimmer of hope that my life has value.

At this point in the journal process, you should have five days of journal notes to review. That is five days of value that you have added to your life. If you have become honest with yourself, you now have your honest opinion to draw from. This journal is the person you have become over the last five days. You have become honest with yourself and have put aside your suicidal thoughts for the previous five days. Take council in your journal by using your own words to find value in your life. If you take your life, you will no longer have it, and you can never get it back. Be warned that you are weak and in need of help. At the very least, you will need to continue to journal, reading, and re-reading your thoughts. Just because you made it to day five or day six doesn't mean that you can't go back to your darkest hour. Press on and add value to your life every day through honesty and truth.

John 15:26 But when the Helper comes, whom I shall send to you from the Father, the Spirit of truth who proceeds from the Father, He will testify of Me.

Remember, suicide is an act of a person intentionally taking their own life. If the act of suicide is never started, then the act of suicide can never be finished. Life moves on, move along with it, and begin to direct your path in honesty and truth. The new beginning starts here and now.

Discussion Questions: none.

Scriptures: John 15:22 [KJV], John 1:1, John 6:57, John 15:26.

The next step is to seek professional help.

National Suicide Prevention lifeline: 1-800-273-8255

Made in the USA
Columbia, SC
14 April 2021